FAT
QUARTERS

A Quilters Club Mystery

FAT QUARTERS

A Quilters Club Mystery

Marjorie Sorrell Rockwell

ABSOLUTELY AMAZING eBOOKS

ABSOLUTELY AMAZING eBOOKS

Published by Whiz Bang LLC, 926 Truman Avenue, Key West, Florida 33040, USA.

For information contact:
Publisher@AbsolutelyAmazingEbooks.com

ISBN-13: 978-1945772825 (Absolutely Amazing Ebooks)
ISBN-10: 1945772824

When feeling low, it's time to sew.

Other Quilters Club Mysteries
By Marjory Sorrell Rockwell

A Christmas Quit (Prequel)

The Quilters Club Quartet

The Quilters Club Trio

The Underhanded Stitch

The Patchwork Puzzler

Coming Unraveled

Hemmed In

Sewed Up Tight

All Tangled Up

Needled

Stitch In Time

Cross Stitch

Available from
<u>AbsolutelyAmazingEbooks.com</u>

FAT
QUARTERS

A Quilters Club Mystery

PART 1

CHAPTER ONE
The UFO

MADDY MADISON SAW A UFO. No, not a flying saucer. She didn't believe in little green men. After all, she was a sensible 60-year-old woman living in Caruthers Corners, a quiet little town in northeastern Indiana. Far from strange aerial phenomenon or unexplained lights in the sky.

What she saw was probably a comet or a weather balloon or sunlight reflecting off an airplane. At least, that's what she told her gal pals at next Tuesday's meeting. The members of the Quilters Club kept few secrets from each other.

Maddy's granddaughter Aggie saw the UFO too. "A seagull," she declared, being a sensible 15-year-old. But Gruesome Gorge State Park was a good 680 miles from the ocean.

The state park, that's where Maddy and Aggie had been when they spotted the Unidentified Flying Object that Sunday afternoon. They'd been there to pick up Aggie's cousin, N'yen. The boy had spent the weekend camping with his troop, the Badger Patrol. Indiana didn't have an official state animal, but if it did the choice no doubt would be between a badger and a bobcat.

"It was probably the aurora borealis," N'yen shrugged. Scanning the afternoon sky for any sign of a UFO.

"Aurora what?" said Aggie Tidemore. Although a

clever girl, she had little interest in meteorological matters.

"Aurora Borealis," N'yen explained. "Auroras are produced when the magnetosphere is disturbed by solar winds, charging electron and proton particles in the thermosphere where the energy is precipitated due to the Earth's magnetic field. That causes the lights in the sky." Her cousin was turning into a genuine Brainiac.

"Pshaw," said his grandmother. "This isn't Nome, Alaska. We don't see northern lights down here in Indiana. This is not exactly a prime site for solar light shows."

"Auroras are occasionally visible in lower latitudes," N'yen stuck to his assessment. "Especially when a geomagnetic storm temporarily enlarges the auroral oval."

"Is that so?"

"Large geomagnetic storms are most common during the peak of the 11-year sunspot cycle. We're at the tail-end of one now."

"How do you know all this?" asked Maddy.

"I read," he said.

Maddy rolled her eyes as she loaded his canvas backpack into the rear of her blue Toyota Sequoia. "What we saw was an object in the sky, not the northern lights," she insisted.

"You're saying it was a flying saucer?" the boy scoffed. Now that he was thirteen, he was becoming more mouthy. But he was a good kid at heart, happy to be living with his Grampy and Grammy, only a block or so from his cousin Aggie's house. N'yen and Aggie were best-est of friends. Had been since they met, shortly after his adoption by her Uncle Bill and Aunt Kathy. He'd lost his Vietnamese parents in a car accident.

"Let's just call it an unidentified flying object," Maddy replied with a sheepish smile.

"I still say it was a seagull," Aggie persisted. The girl squinted into the blue bowl of the sky, hoping for another glimpse.

But what she saw was a low-flying airplane. A door on the passenger side had been removed. As she watched, a skydiver tumbled out of the plane, plummeting toward the Earth like an apple falling from a tree.

"Whoa," she said. "Look at that."

"What?" Maddy looked up, thinking the girl had spotted another UFO.

"That plane's too low for skydiving," observed N'yen.

True to the boy's words, the figure in the sky continued its downward trajectory, chute not opening.

"Oh my," breathed Maddy, as the falling figure disappeared into the ragged treeline of Never Ending Swamp. Realizing they had likely witnessed a man's death.

"The parachute didn't open," said Aggie, aghast at what she had seen.

"Quick," said her grandmother. "Call your Uncle Freddie at the Fire Department. Tell him to send a paramedic unit. I'll call the Police Department and ask Jim to put together a search party." Her friend Jim Purdue was the town's police chief, but in practice he and his men served the entire county, there being no sheriff.

"Nobody could have survived that fall," said Aggie, hurriedly pressing buttons on her iPhone.

"Maybe the trees broke his fall," speculated her cousin N'yen. But he sounded doubtful.

"Let's hope so," Maddy patted her grandson's shoulder. But her words didn't convey much hope.

"You don't jump out of an airplane and survive," said Aggie after she had called the fire department for paramedics.

"Especially without a parachute," commented N'yen.

"His chute didn't open," said Aggie.

"No, he wasn't wearing a parachute," her cousin clarified. He had 20/20 vision.

"No chute?" gasped Maddy Madison.

"No chute," the boy repeated.

"Then," said his grandmother, "that makes it one of three things: A horrible accident, suicide, or murder."

"Good gravy," said Aggie, "this sounds like a job for the Quilters Club."

CHAPTER TWO
Murder In the Sky

THE QUILTERS CLUB was a small needlecraft group that met once a week at the Hoople Quilting Heritage Museum. There were only four members – five if you counted Aggie. Or six if you added N'yen. Even though the boy didn't do any quilting, he considered himself an auxiliary member.

In addition to Madelyn Madison, the confab consisted of Lizzie Ridenour, the fussy redhead who oversaw the new quilting museum; Cookie Brown, the brainy blonde in charge of the Caruthers Corners Historical Society; and Bootsie Purdue, the pudgy brunette who had just been voted president-elect of the sprawling no-kill animal shelter on the edge of town.

They were prominent citizens of this tiny Midwestern town – population 3,154 – not just because of their numerous civic activities, but also due to their families' positions in local society: Maddy's hubby, a former mayor, was descended from a Town Founder; Lizzie was married to a former bank president; Cookie's husband was a well-to-do farmer involved with the town zoo; and Bootsie was wife of the chief of police.

However, all this social whoop-dee-doodle was overshadowed by their growing reputation as amateur sleuths.

Many folks thought of the Quilters Club as an unofficial detective agency. Aside from stitching splendid patchwork quilts, the group had solved a number of local mysteries – from lost boys to haunted houses, stolen dinosaur bones to Russian spies. An impressive array for a town that was little more than a flyspeck on a roadmap.

Now they were gathered in the workroom of the Quilting Museum for their regular Tuesday meeting. Aggie and N'yen were there too.

Under Lizzie's tutelage, Aggie was becoming a first-rate quilter. She'd just placed second in the junior quilting competition at Watermelon Days. That was an annual fair based on the area's main agricultural product – watermelons.

As for N'yen, he just came along for the ride, usually sitting quietly in the corner playing "Tower Duel" on his iPad. A challenging multiplayer tower defense game, he'd lately been competing online with an almost impossible-to-beat player known as Beelzebub666. "The Devil," N'yen called his opponent.

"Any word on the jumper?" Maddy asked.

"They found the body this morning," reported Bootsie. As the police chief's wife, she had an insider's pipeline to such facts.

"Dead?" asked Lizzie.

"Every splatter of him."

"Ugh!"

N'yen looked up from his game. "The median height for death from falls is 50 feet. That's the equivalent of 4 to 5 stories. Few people survive at that distance."

"My Uncle Tommy died from falling off a stepladder," volunteered Lizzie. "He was pretty clumsy."

"Have they identified the jumper yet?" asked

Cookie. As director of the Caruthers Corners Historical Society, she knew most local genealogies by heart. Likely she would be familiar with the victim's family.

"Nope. But they've sent the fingerprints off to the FBI for identification."

Maddy looked up from the fat quarter she was working on, a needle poised in her hand. "What a horrible sight it was, watching that poor man going down, down, down."

"He went down like a rock," nodded her granddaughter. She was working on a Log Cabin quilt, a repeated single block pattern representing the walls of an old-timey log cabin. A red center patch denoted the cabin's hearth or fire.

"Falling objects accelerate at 32 feet per second per second," noted N'yen.

"Watchoo talkin' 'bout Willis?" said Aggie – parroting the catch phrase from that old *Different Strokes* TV show. She was super smart, but physics was not her forte.

N'yen ignored his cousin's sassiness. "The formula for determining the velocity of a falling object is $v_f = g * t$ where t is time and g is the acceleration of gravity," the boy explained. It seemed so simple to him.

Aggie rolled her eyes. "Things fall faster and faster, you mean?"

"That's what I said."

"Well, that accounts for the splat," Bootsie translated the boy's words into practical terms. Accurate but not pretty.

"Forget about the dead guy. Tell us more about the flying saucer," urged Lizzie.

The redhead was a big *X-Files* fan. She liked watching Scully and Mulder search for the Truth Out There. She'd been thrilled when they brought the *X-Files* series back to TV.

"It wasn't a flying saucer," Maddy corrected the redhead. "It was a UFO, an unidentified flying object."

"It *could've* been a flying saucer," argued Lizzie. "You can't be sure. That's why it's called 'unidentified.'"

"I think it was a seagull," interjected Aggie.

"A turkey buzzard perhaps," said Cookie. "There are no seagulls around here. Other than a little stretch along Lake Michigan, we're a landlocked state."

"Actually thirty-one species of gulls have been recorded in Indiana," offered N'yen. He was smart. The kids at school called him Encyclopedia Brown, after that brainy character in the HBO TV series.

"So your UFO was a bird?" asked Bootsie.

"Maybe it was just sunlight reflecting off that airplane we saw," suggested Maddy. An Ellen Burstyn lookalike, she had recently let her hair go silver. It was "quite becoming," in her hairdresser's words. She was still trying to make up her mind whether she liked it or not.

"What kind of plane was it?" asked Cookie. "A prop plane? A private jet? A commercial airliner?"

"It was a Cessna Turbo 172 Skyhawk JT-A," said N'yen.

"A Cessna what?"

"A diesel-powered fixed-wing aircraft," the boy clarified. "Skydivers, judging by that missing door. Jumpers sometimes remove them to make it easier to clear the plane's fuselage."

Cookie was working on the hem of a Jelly Roll quilt. "Who did the Cessna belong to? Find the pilot, you'll likely identify the jumper."

"The police haven't found the plane yet," said Bootsie, inspecting the progress on her own quilt, an Amish Sunshine and Shadows design. This part of Indiana had more Amish than any other place in America, except for Lancaster, Pennsylvania.

"Why not?" Lizzie wanted to know. "Don't planes have to file a flight plan?"

Bootsie shook her head, barely ruffling her brunette pixie cut. "Airplanes taking off from private airstrips don't always file a flight plan, especially for skydiving or joyriding."

"Joyriding!" exclaimed Maddy. "Tell that to the guy who fell out."

"You mean got pushed," said Aggie.

That was a conversation stopper.

~ ~ ~

Beauregard Hollingsworth Madison IV – Maddy's husband – was off fishing with Lizzie's spouse. Edgar Ridenour had a flat-bottomed boat suitable for shallow spots along the Wabash. During the 19th Century the river had been an important route for steamships carrying passengers and cargo, but silt from farming runoffs eventually clogged the bottom, making it all but impassable.

However, the catfish and bass were plentiful for fishermen.

Stretching across Indiana, the 503-mile-long waterway was originally called *Ouabache*, an Algonquin word for "water over white stones." Maybe it had been like that at one time, but today its muddy waters were dark and meandering.

Being the official state river of Indiana, the Wabash had inspired the song "On the Banks of the Wabash, Far Away." Written in 1897 by Paul Dresser, the best-selling ditty earned the songwriter more than $100,000 in sheet-music sales. Those were the days.

Beau and Edgar usually went fishing on weekends, but this Tuesday's foray was a special occasion – the tenth anniversary of Edgar's early retirement as president of Caruthers Corners Savings & Loan.

Embracing this free time with great enthusiasm, he'd packed away his Gieves & Hawkes tailor-made business suits (being an Anglophile, he preferred this tony Savile Row tailor) and bought an outdoorsy new wardrobe from Duluth Traders. He quit shaving and let his hair grow long. He could have passed for a Jeremiah Johnson type mountain man. Fishing was now his life.

His wife didn't mind. She and Edgar lead fairly separate existences. Not exactly a marriage of convenience, but it had started off as a fusion of his financial ambitions and her family's ownership of the Savings & Loan. Nicolas Bergamachi, Lizzie's Italian-born grandfather, had founded the bank in the mid-1800s. She still held the controlling stock.

Edgar gave Beau Madison credit for encouraging his break with the corporate world. Sure, Edgar still served on a few boards (the Savings & Loan, Burpyville Memorial, and such), but he valued not having to wear a white shirt and striped power tie to work every day. The starch had irritated his neck.

Yes, he was an ardent admirer of the British, but his interest veered more toward British outdoorsmen like Lieutenant-General Robert Stephenson Smyth Baden-Powell, Sir Francis Edward Younghusband, Edward James Corbett, Sir Ranulph Fiennes, and Sir Christian John Storey Bonington.

Inspired by camper organizations like the Boys Brigade and the Woodcraft Indians, Baden-Powell had founded the Boy Scouts Association as well as the Girl Guides. In the same way, Edgar Ridenour became a big supporter of the Sons of Anthony Wayne, a statewide camping organization designed for Indiana youths. "Mad Anthony" was the hero of the Battle of Fallen Timbers, the first skirmish in the Northwest Indian War (1785–1795). Nearby Fort Wayne was named after him.

The Badger Patrol was the local branch of Sons of Anthony Wayne. It claimed twelve members, all of them boys. Ben Bentley was the troop leader.

Aggie Tidemore led a protest against this sexist attitude, despite her cousin N'yen being a full-fledged Lieutenant Colonel in the organization. Cookie Bentley's husband held the title of Brigadier General. Ben had been attempting to form a Dolly Madison wing, but that wasn't good enough for a budding feminist like Aggie. She was threatening to write a letter of complaint to Gloria Steinem.

In celebration of the anniversary of Edgar's retirement, Beau Madison had brought along a bottle of Dom Aitkens Brut, a faux champagne bottled by Boyd Aitkens's small winery on the north end of the county. The vineyard was a hobby of Aitkens, his main business being growing Charleston Greys and Black Diamonds, two popular varieties of picnic melons. Over 6 percent of all watermelons grown in the US come from Indiana.

"Bottoms up," saluted Beau, clinking his 6 oz. plastic cup against Edgar's, sloshing a bit of the sparkling wine onto his sleeve in the process.

"Up yours," laughed his friend. It was a pleasant day on the water, floating lazily near the Highway 101 Bridge. This was the habitat of Big Calvin, the legendary catfish once caught and released by Beau's grandson N'yen.

"Any word on that skydiver who landed in Never Ending Swamp?" asked Beau, just to be making conversation. He was always amazed how his wife wound up in the middle of most things mysterious here in Caruthers Corners.

"Jim said they located the guy's remains this morning." Beau and Edgar and Jim and Ben had been buds in high school. All had married their high school girlfriends, though it took Ben a while to hook up with Cookie. There had been a slight detour with her first husband, another member of their crowd. Bob's demise in a freak tractor accident opened the door for Ben Bentley's return to favor.

"The skydiver's chute didn't open?"

Edgar downed his drink. "Wasn't wearing a chute. Just like N'yen said."

"N'yen's got good eyesight."

"That's not all. The boy has become quite the polymath."

Beau followed suit, emptying his cup. "A poly-what?"

Edgar chuckled. He was an accomplished wordsmith – fishing and reading being his primary pastimes. "That's a person whose expertise spans a significant number of different subject areas."

"A know-it-all?"

"Fact is, N'yen *does* know it all. A polymath draws on complex bodies of knowledge to solve specific problems."

Beau nodded, picking up his fishing rod. "Sounds like him."

"That boy's come a long way since he moved in with you and Maddy." A year or so ago Bill Madison and his wife had gone through a bad divorce, turning over custody of their adopted son to Bill's parents.

"Gotta admit I wasn't sure how it would work out," nodded Beau. He'd served in the Vietnam War, an Army grunt more used to having short Asians in pajamas shooting at him than calling him "Grampy."

"I think being 'parents' again has been good for you and Maddy," said Edgar. His own two daughters had not turned out so well, neither of them speaking to him and Liz these days. Married now, they had lives of their own.

Beau ran his fingers through his graying hair. "It's been wonderful. N'yen and Aggie are like having kids again." Aggie spent so much time at her grandparents' house you'd think she lived there.

"Truth is, I've become quite fond of the little rapscallion," said Edgar. "He's turned into a great fishing partner for you and me."

Beau chuckled. "He *did* catch Big Calvin."

"I do hold that against him," the ex-banker joked with a deadpan expression.

"Why would that skydiver jump out of a plane without a parachute?" Beau changed the subject. "That's plum crazy."

"Maybe he was committing suicide."

"If that were true, wouldn't the pilot come forward with the story?"

"An accident then?"

"Again, where's the pilot?"

"Maybe the pilot thought he was somehow at fault. Keeping his mouth shut."

"Maybe, but you'd think he would do the right thing."

"Then that leaves the last choice – murder."

"Hmm. That might explain why the pilot has disappeared."

CHAPTER THREE
Flying High

MADDY AND HER QUILTERS CLUB CRONIES reached the same conclusion – that the pilot of the Cessna 172 Skyhawk had pushed his passenger out without a parachute. According to eagle-eyed N'yen, there was no one else in the four-seater fixed-wing aircraft. *Ergo*, the pilot had to be the murderer.

During 2016, the United States Parachute Association recorded only 21 skydiving deaths in the US. That was also the same number of deaths as in 2015 and slightly below the average for the last 10 years. Skydiving fatalities account for about .0075 deaths per 1,000 jumps. You're actually safer than riding on a bus.

But not if you aren't wearing a parachute.

The typical cruising altitude for a Cessna 172 is 4,000 to 6,000 feet. At that height you can enjoy the scenery. However, the standard jump altitude is 12,000 feet above ground level. That's one turn of the standard parachutist's altimeter. That altitude is within easy reach of a Cessna with a standard engine. It doesn't even require supplementary oxygen (needed if you fly more than 30 minutes at 12,500 feet or higher).

The plane they had seen was flying low. N'yen estimated it at about 3,000 feet. Some people have survived falling from that altitude. The guy who fell out of the Cessna had not been so lucky.

Survival at even higher altitudes *is* possible. The Guinness World Record goes to a Serbian flight attendant who fell 33,330 feet without a parachute – and lived. Her fall took place after an explosion tore through the baggage compartment of JAT Flight 367 on January 26, 1972, causing it to crash near Srbská Kamenice, Czechoslovakia.

But then again, some people die falling off the roof of a one-story house.

"We need to find that pilot," Maddy Madison reiterated. "He's the murderer, no question about that." The Quilters Club had gathered in her kitchen that Wednesday morning to plan their investigation. Bootsie's husband would have blown a gasket if he'd known these "meddlesome females" were at it again, interfering with an ongoing police investigation.

"To do that, we need to find the plane," stated Cookie Bentley. She had a logical mind. Rarely could anyone argue with her pronouncements.

Bootsie Purdue spoke up, between bites of watermelon pie. Her favorite. "The police have checked airports in a six-state area. Nada so far."

"A Cessna Turbo Skyhawk JT-A is powered by a 155-horsepower diesel engine," shrugged N'yen, as if stating a commonly known fact. "It can travel nearly 1,000 miles without landing to refuel."

"Oh my. That's the distance from here to Dallas, Texas," said Cookie, showing off her near-eidetic memory. "A six-state search area isn't a big enough circle."

"To be fair, there's no way a small town police department can cover an area that large," said Bootsie, sounding like an apologist for her husband's efforts.

"How about the FBI?" suggested Lizzie, inspecting her lipstick in a compact mirror. A shade called Russet Sunset, it matched her red hair.

"The FBI doesn't have authority to investigate local murders," replied Bootsie. "Not unless it involves a Hate Crime or something like that."

"How about the FAA or the NTSB?" suggested N'yen.

"What's that?" asked Lizzie, confused by all this alphabet soup – FBI, FAA, NTSN.

"The Federal Aviation Administration and the National Transportation Safety Board," Cookie clarified. "They have jurisdiction over air transportation."

"That's an interesting thought," said Maddy.

Aggie quickly Googled 'National Transportation Safety Board' on her iPhone. "Says here, the NTSB investigates any 'occurrence associated with the operation of an aircraft which takes place between the time any person boards the aircraft with the intention of flight and all such persons have disembarked, in which any person suffers death or serious injury....' " The girl was quoting from an online document titled *The NTSB's Role in Aviation Safety*.

"That sounds promising," observed Maddy. Cutting herself another slice of watermelon pie.

"Me too, me too," begged N'yen, eyeing the pie.

"Aggie?" asked her grandmother.

"Yes, please."

Bootsie studied the pie. "As long as you're cutting new slices," she said, holding out her plate. Knowing she'd never lose that extra 20 pounds at this rate.

~ ~ ~

Evoking the FAA or NTSB required a far greater authority than the Quilters Club. So later that morning the four women and two teens found themselves sitting across the conference table from Police Chief Purdue and Mayor Tidemore on the second floor of the Caruthers Corners Town Hall.

Jim Purdue glared at his wife. Obviously irked that Bootsie and her cronies had outflanked him by getting the mayor involved. Mark Tidemore was, of course, Maddy's son-in-law and Aggie's father. Stacking the deck in their favor.

Jim knew the meeting wouldn't go well for him when Mark started it off by winking at Aggie and saying, "Hi, Sugar Plum. You and N'yen want to go down to the Dairy Queen for a Blizzard after we finish here?"

"Yes, Daddy," beamed the blonde girl.

"Oh boy," grinned her Asian cousin.

Mark Tidemore looked around the table, nodding at his guests. "Now what brings the Quilters Club out today?"

Cookie spoke up, it having been decided she had less conflict than Maddy or Bootsie. And was more focused than Lizzie, who tended to be a bit ditzy. "As you know, Maddy and your daughter saw the man fall out of that plane on Sunday. But the pilot hasn't come forward. We thought it might be a good idea to ask the Federal Aviation Administration or the National Transportation Safety Board to help locate the plane."

"A Cessna Turbo 172 Skyhawk JT-A," volunteered

the boy.

"We have that in the report," said Chief Purdue. "You didn't happen to get the plane's markings, did you?"

"No, I don't have a photographic memory like Aunt Cookie." Technically, Cookie, Bootsie, and Lizzie were not aunts, but N'yen and Aggie treated them as if they were. "But it had a number beginning with N."

"All private planes have registrations beginning with N," said the Police Chief.

In accordance with the Convention on International Civil Aviation, the National Aviation Authority allocates a unique alphanumeric string to identify each aircraft. It's commonly called an "N" number, because all aircraft registered in the United States are assigned a number beginning with the letter N. This identifier must be displayed on a civilian plane's fuselage.

"I don't remember the number either," blurted Aggie.

"Nor I," said Maddy. "But surely there can't be that many Cessnas to chase down."

"You'd be surprised. There've been more Cessna 172 Skyhawks built than any other aircraft," replied Chief Purdue, demonstrating that he'd done his homework. "As of 2015, Cessna and its partners have sold over 44,000 of these single-engine, fixed-wing planes. Even more by now."

"Yes, but there aren't that many Skyhawk JT-A models," countered N'yen. He'd done his homework too. "It wasn't certified until 2017, so not that many have been sold."

"A good point," the mayor nodded.

"Another thing," added the boy, "with a Continental CD-155 diesel engine, the JT-A carries a hefty price tag – $450,000. That's a third more costly than a Cessna 172-R. A price like that would likely depress sales."

"True," agreed the mayor.

Jim Purdue wasn't about to give up easily. "How can you be sure the plane you guys saw was a Skyhawk JT-A instead of a 172-SP or 172-L or 172-R? There's a ton of different models."

N'yen smiled, impressed by Uncle Jim's familiarity with Cessna models. "You're right," he agreed. "There are a lot of different models. Cessna started with the 172 followed by the 172-A and continued sequentially up to 172-S, with the exception of the J and O which never got certified. Those planes all look pretty much the same. But the Turbo 172 Skyhawk JT-A is recognizable by the stylized design on its fuselage."

"What design?"

"Y' know, blue speed lines like you'd see in a *Flash* comic book."

"Oh." Jim Purdue was working to follow the boy's words.

"Also turbo engines sound different. Not as noisy as ordinary Cessnas."

"That so?" The Police Chief didn't have much of a comeback.

"I'm pretty sure the plane we saw was a Turbo 172 Skyhawk JT-A. I've been reading up on them recently. I'm thinking about taking up skydiving."

"N'yen!" shrieked his grandmother. "You're much

too young to be jumping out of airplanes. Didn't you just see what can happen?"

"I'd be wearing a parachute," he said as if that clarified everything.

"Who put that crazy idea in your head?" asked Lizzie, horrified by the idea.

N'yen didn't answer, merely ducking his head.

"Uncle Freddie did," said Aggie. "Remember, he was an Airborne Ranger in Desert Storm. He's offered to take N'yen skydiving, but he won't let me go with them."

"Neither of you are going skydiving," said Maddy firmly. "I used to worry myself to death when Freddie was in jump school." Her son had always been a thrill seeker, fueled by adrenaline. Maybe that's why he became a firefighter after serving his four years in the Army. Now he was covered in burn scars to prove it. While working for the Atlanta Fire Rescue Department he'd suffered second-degree burns on 30% of his body, leaving him looking like the creature in a cheap horror movie.

"Tattletale," said the boy, casting a dirty look at his cousin.

"I prefer to think of myself as a whistleblower," sniffed Aggie. "Maybe next time you and Uncle Freddie will think twice before not including me."

"Agnes Millicent Tidemore," said her father sternly, "you will *not* be jumping out of any airplanes."

"D-dad."

"About the FAA," Chief Purdue tried to get back to the subject at hand. "I'll check with them and see what they can do to help us find that Cessna 172."

"The Cessna Turbo 172 Skyhawk JT-A," corrected N'yen. Being precise.

"*Any* Cessna that might have been flying in this area on Sunday will do," said the Chief. Trying to sound authoritative.

"I'm not so sure the FAA can pinpoint a Cessna out for a Sunday flight," the Mayor shook his head. "Do they track private planes that closely?"

Chief Purdue sighed. "We'll find out."

But they didn't get that far. The pilot turned up the very next day.

CHAPTER FOUR
Upside Down Lou

FREDDIE MADISON GOT AN EARFUL that night when he and Amanda and their two kids came over to dinner. Freddie had been lured over by the promise of watermelon stew, one of his childhood favorites. Little did he know that he was stepping into a steel-toothed bear trap set by his mother.

Freddie was the middle child, a few years younger than brother Bill, a few years older than sister Tilly. Bill, of course, was N'yen's adoptive dad; Tilly was Aggie's mom. The two brothers had a testy relationship. Picking no sides, Tilly idolized both of them.

As a working fireman in Atlanta, Freddie had been badly burned in an apartment-building conflagration. His chances of survival fifty-fifty. But after a few years of recuperation, he'd been eager to return to work. Horribly scarred, he had to get used to looking more like the Freddy Krueger in the mirror than the once-handsome Freddie Madison he remembered.

Having returned to his hometown, he'd been hired as Fire Chief when ol' Pete Watson retired. He'd had an inside track, his brother-in-law being the Mayor.

Nonetheless, it was a high-pressure job, fighting house fires and other blazes. To relieve the stress, he had recently taken up skydiving. He'd always enjoyed making jumps when in the Airborne Rangers.

However, his offer to teach 13-year-old N'yen had

been the wrong move.

"Freddie, how could you," his mother said the moment he stepped in the door. "Are you trying to kill yourself and N'yen too?"

"Huh?"

"Don't play dumb with me," she said, ushering her son and his family into the kitchen. They'd been twenty minutes late, and the watermelon stew was already on the table. But it hadn't been sitting there for the entire twenty minutes, for Freddie noticed it was still piping hot.

Everybody took their places, Beau and the children knowing the safest way to survive this conversation between mother and son was to say nothing. Freddie's wife and adopted daughter Donna took the cue. Baby Tess was still sleeping in her mother's arms, oblivious to the hubbub going on around the table.

"What's the bee in your bonnet, Mom?" asked Freddie as his mother ladled out the stew. Freshly baked bread was on the table. Chocolate cornstarch pudding was waiting on the counter for dessert. Maddy Madison didn't mete out punishment without a hardy meal for the condemned.

"You were going to take N'yen skydiving!" she continued, more calmly.

"Who told you that?" He glanced at the boy.

"Wasn't me," N'yen responded meekly. "Aggie squealed on us."

Freddie turned his gaze toward his niece. She'd been invited for dinner tonight, her parents having driven down to Burpyville to catch a movie. Some Bruce Willis film deemed too violent for the kids. They had a babysitter for the younger two.

"Don't blame Aggie," his mother said. "You're the guilty party here. Your brother Bill would never approve of you teaching N'yen how to jump out of an airplane. For that matter, neither would your father nor I."

"Well, I –" Beauregard Madison began to speak, but cut off his words when Maddy gave him the ol' stink eye.

"Like I said," she continued, "you had no business planning something dangerous like that with your nephew."

"I was going to ask you first. He and I were just talking –"

"– about jumping out of an airplane at 12,000 feet," she accused.

"Yes, but –"

"Don't give me any excuses, Frederic Hollingsworth Madison. You've crossed the line on this one."

Beau reached across the table and patted his wife's hand. The gesture seemed to calm her down, like soothing a skittish mare. "Now, now," he said quietly, "you're just upset at seeing that guy fall out an airplane the other day. A delayed reaction."

"It was terrible," she sniffled.

Freddie got up and came around the table to give his mom a hug. "Don't worry," he said as he buried his face against her silver hair. "I'd never do anything like that behind your back."

"Maybe I am overwrought from watching that poor fellow jump to his death."

"He was pushed," N'yen corrected her.

"You're right," she sighed. "It's just hard to believe."

"The pilot has to be the murderer," reasoned Aggie, happy to turn the conversation away from the subject of who squealed on whom. "Nobody else could have done it. There were only two people in that airplane."

"That's right," confirmed N'yen. "Nobody but the pilot and the skydiver."

"Skydiver?" said Freddie's wife, trying to follow the conversation.

"I'm pretty sure they were supposed to be skydiving," nodded the boy as he sipped at the stew. "The door had been removed from the co-pilot side."

"That's because it's not easy to jump out of a Cessna 172 with a standard door," confirmed Freddie. "The slip stream makes it difficult to open."

Aggie said, "What kind of plane do you jump out of, Uncle Freddie?"

"Usually a Cessna 182. Its door is hinged on top, making the exit easier."

"Maybe the FCC will locate the plane," sighed Maddy.

"It could be anywhere in a thousand mile radius," Beau reminded her.

"I kinda doubt that," said Freddie. "With a door removed, it probably came from someplace fairly close."

"Besides," added N'yen, "skydivers would never fly a thousand miles to reach a Drop Zone." Freddie had been tutoring him well.

"Drop Zone?" exclaimed Maddy. "That plane was

flying over Never Ending Swamp."

"If you were going to kill somebody, that would be a good place to do it," observed Aggie. "Nobody would ever find the body in there."

"My men found it – well, most of it," said Freddie.

"That's only because witnesses saw the body fall out of the plane," Beau pointed out. "If Maddy and the kids hadn't been there, nobody would have known to go looking in the swamp."

Beau Madison was right. Never Ending Swamp was 400 acres of bog, trees, and quicksand, a no-man's land located just north of town on Highway 102. The swamp was the site where three local boys disappeared back in 1982. Few people ventured inside its deadly parameters without good reason.

"True. My men never would've stumbled across the remains if you hadn't pointed us to the southeast quadrant of the swamp. We had to keep in sight of each other, else we might've gotten lost. As it was, we had to mark our trail every ten feet."

"Like Hansel and Gretel leaving breadcrumbs," said Little Donna. She was in kindergarten now.

"Well, kinda like that, sweetie," smiled Freddie, making his scarred face look ghastly, like a Halloween mask. But his daughter was used to him, and merely giggled, proud of her observation. She was big on fairy tales these days.

"A local skydiver, you think?" Maddy returned to the subject at hand.

"Most likely."

"But he wasn't wearing a chute," Aggie reminded them.

"Maybe he hadn't put it on, not being near a Drop Zone."

"So where would a local skydiver come from?" asked his mother.

Freddie shrugged as he refilled his bowl with stew. "There might be some strips over near Indianapolis. But the only place I know is the Head in the Clouds Skydiving School at Burpyville. That's where I fly out of. Lou Ritchie is my instructor. He's got a plain-vanilla Cessna 182."

"Lou Ritchie," Beau mulled over the name. "Don't think I know him."

"People call him Upside Down Lou. He used to be a stunt pilot."

"I'm sure Chief Purdue checked out your skydiving school," said Maddy. "But he didn't find anyone with a Cessna Turbo Seahawk."

"*Sky*hawk," N'yen corrected.

Freddie cocked his head, as if thinking. "The Cessna Turbo is a diesel engine. It uses Jet-A fuel. Lou doesn't have that. Most Cessnas or Cirruses or Pipers take Avgas."

"Oh well, that's a dead end," said Maddy. Having completely forgotten her anger at her son. "Here, dear. Have some more watermelon stew."

"Thank, Mom."

Beau said, "Commercial airliners use jet fuel. Any skydivers fly out of the Burpyville Regional Airport?"

"Not as a rule," said Freddie. "Most use Lou's strip. But if you owned a Cessna Turbo I guess you'd have to."

"Wouldn't the police have found one if it was there?" asked Maddy. "I'm sure they checked the regional airport too."

"Depends on who you talk with," Freddie said between bites of stew. "The private hangars are off to the side, away from the commercial airliners. Professional pilots and their crews don't usually mingle much with civilian pilots."

Beau wrinkled his brow. "Who'd know if there's a Cessna Turbo sitting in a private hangar over there?"

"I could ask Lou. He hangs out with the civilian pilots. He used to work out of the regional airport before he got his own strip."

"Could you call him now, Uncle Freddie?" pressed Aggie. She could be very OCD sometimes.

He glanced up at the quartz clock on the kitchen wall. 8:15, the hands said. "I guess it's not too late to call. But he may be out playing poker with his buds. I can't remember whether it's Wednesday or Thursday that's his poker night."

"Go ahead," encouraged Maddy. A tad OCD herself.

Freddie walked over to the wall phone, looked in his wallet for a business card for the skydiving school, and dialed a number. The phone rang for a full minute before someone answered.

"Head In the Clouds Skydiving."

"Lou, that you?"

"Yeah. Who's this?"

"Freddie. Freddie Madison."

"Oh, the fire chief over in Caruthers Corners."

"That's right. Got a question to ask."

"Fire away," Upside Down Lou chuckled, pleased with his wordplay.

"Do you know anyone who has a Cessna Turbo 172 Skyhawk JT-A over at the regional airport?"

"Sure do," said Lou.

"Who?"

"Me."

CHAPTER FIVE
Separated at Birth

THE QUILTERS CLUB – the adult members, that is – met for breakfast at Cozy Café, the diner on South Main Street owned by Maddy's twin sister. Maddy and Maisie Walters had known each other all their lives, but only recently discovered that they were related. At birth their unwed mother had given them both up for adoption to two different families.

The two women had little in common, other than the same genetic heritage and fat trust funds established by the Hoople Quadruplets foundation. Their father had been one of the Hoople Quadruples, as they were called, at one time the town's most famous citizens. Now only Aunt Hilda remained, alone up there in that big stone mansion atop Hoople Hill.

Maisie was single; Maddy was married. Maisie's hair was dyed jet-black; Maddy's now silver. Being fraternal twins, they looked nothing alike. Not knowing they were related, they'd traveled in different circles in high school. Maddy went off to college with her pals; Maisie became a waitress at Cozy Café.

Now, Maisie owned the joint.

And Maddy was donating money to philanthropic causes.

All thanks to the new trust funds set by Hilda Hoople when their birth secret was revealed last year. A Welcome to the Family gift, so to speak.

This particular morning Maddy and Cookie and

Bootsie and Lizzie crowded into the corner booth, a little tight since Bootsie was off her diet. Maisie brought four cups of piping hot coffee over without being asked.

"We got watermelon waffles this morning," she advised. "Or there's the scrambled eggs special. Both $3.99 including coffee."

It wasn't a hard choice – waffles all around.

"We located the pilot," Maddy announced after everyone had a sip of coffee to get the blood pumping.

"Do tell," said Lizzie. "Did he confess?"

"We don't know yet," replied Bootsie. "Jim sent a deputy out to arrest him early this morning. We haven't heard back."

"Who is he?" asked Cookie.

"A guy named Louis Ritchie. They call him Upside Down Lou."

"Doesn't sound like someone I'd want to fly with," observed Lizzie. Sipping her coffee carefully, so as not to smudge her lipstick. Today's shade was called Rosetta Red.

"Apparently he used to be a stunt flyer," Maddy explained. "You know, loop-de-loops and barrel rolls."

"And upside down, I take it," said Lizzie. Suppressing a laugh. The idea was ridiculous, flying upside down.

"Ritchie," Cookie repeated the name. "I know the family. His mother was a Crackleton."

"Good gravy," Bootsie rolled her eyes. "I sure wouldn't want to go flying with a Crackleton." Everybody knew that the inhabitants of Crackleton Crossing were "cuckoo for Cocoa Puffs," thanks to all the clan's inbreeding.

"Maybe one of these days crazy ol' Granny Crackleton will tell where the Jinks gold is buried," laughed Lizzie. Local legend had it that one of the Town Founders, Ferdinand Aloysius Jinks, had buried a wagonload of gold hereabouts.

"She doesn't have to," confided Maddy *sotto voce*. "I know where to find it."

"Do tell," said Lizzie, having lost interest in her coffee.

"You really know?" asked Bootsie, leaning forward, crowding the booth.

"I think I do," said Maddy. "But I *could* be wrong."

"You're *never* wrong, Madelyn Agnes Hoople Taylor Madison," stated Cookie, eyes gleaming with interest. "Are you going to share with us?"

"The information or the gold?" teased Maddy. Now that she was rich from the Hoople inheritance, a wagonload of gold bars had less appeal than it did to her good friends.

"Both," laughed Cookie.

"I'll settle for the gold," said Bootsie. Being a policeman's wife, she ran the Purdue household on a penny-tight budget.

Lizzie didn't speak up. She was already wealthy, the largess coming from her grandfather who founded the Caruthers Corners Savings & Loan. But thanks to the Hoople money, Maddy and her sister Maisie were now wealthier than Liz Ridenour by far. There might have been a tinge of competitive jealousy on Lizzie's part.

"How did you figure out where to find the Jinks

33

gold?" asked Cookie. Brow wrinkled, a sign of her curiosity.

"You're the one who gave me the clue," Maddy said to the historical society's executive director.

"*Moi*?" responded Cookie. "If I knew, I would have already dug up those gold bars and deposited them in Lizzie's bank."

"Sometimes you don't know what you know," said Maddy, cutting into a watermelon waffle.

~ ~ ~

At that moment, Deputy Pete Hitzer was putting the cuffs on Upside Down Lou. "Sorry to have to do this," he apologized to his prisoner. "But you can't go 'round pushing people outta airplanes."

"Hey, that's what I do for a living," protested Lou Ritchie. "I run a skydiving school."

"Next time you'd better issue your client a parachute. It's a hard landing in Never Ending Swamp without one."

"What the heck you talkin' about? I don't ever fly over that ol' swamp. My Drop Zone is south of here, in a cow pasture down near Amish Acres. I got a deal with Eli Hochstetler, the deacon who runs the place. People gathering at the Drop Zone brings him lotsa business."

As TripAdvisor will tell you, Amish Acres is a touristy version of an Amish village, the centerpiece being a barn-like restaurant that serves family-style meals – dishes like friendship soup, country casserole, pork with dumplings, cream-baked chicken, cabbage rolls, stuffed squash, and apple fried pies. All served family-style at one long table.

"I've had dinner at Amish Acres," said Petie Hitzer.

"Took my mama there for her birthday last month. Sure did like their rhubarb pudding. Had me seconds."

Lou Ritchie cocked his head. "So what's this all about? That fellow who fell out of a plane over Never Ending Swamp?" The story had been in the *Burpyville Gazette* all week.

"*That*'s the very reason," nodded the Deputy. "Witnesses said he was pushed out of a Cessna Turbo. And you're the only person hereabouts who's got one of them."

"Sure, I've got a Cessna Turbo 172 Skyhawk. But it couldn't have been me. I've only owned the plane for two days."

CHAPTER SIX
Dan's Den of Antiquity

AFTER BREAKFAST the four women walked a few doors down from the café to Dan's Den of Antiquity, the town's only antiques shop. For years it had been a repository of all manner of odds and ends: 1920s Barbola Gesso mirrors, handmade Amish furniture, Victorian milk glass shaving sets, Kork Sarouk Persian rugs, German bisque piano baby figurines, Wm Guerin Limoges boxes, and other valuable *objets d'art*.

The proprietor – an elderly Polish immigrant named Daniel Sokolowski – was knowledgeable in all things vintage, collectible, or antique. Several times in the past he had assisted the Quilters Club in solving mysteries. After all, his expertise in rare and historical items was surer than an Internet Google search.

Maddy had suggested they consult with Dan on the missing Jinks gold. Was it likely to be gold bars, as legend had it? Or some other form – nuggets, coins, jewelry? She thought she knew where to look, but not what it might look like.

To their surprise, there was a sign taped to the shop door: CLOSED DUE TO DEATH OF OWNER.

What? Had something happened to their friend?

Bootsie got on her iPhone to call the police station. Her husband would know. Although they were standing only a few steps from the boxy concrete building that served as the Caruthers Corners Police Department, a phone call would be far quicker.

Dispatcher Myrtle Dobbler knew to put the Chief's wife through to him without playing gatekeeper. As Myrtle told her family, "The key to keeping the boss happy is keeping the boss's wife happy."

"Hi, hon?" Jim Purdue answered the phone. "Whatzup?"

"Dan Sokolowski," she said without any amenities. "Has something happened to him?"

"Well, yes. I was just about to call you. The old geezer passed away last night in his sleep. His housekeeper found him this morning. Said he looked as peaceful as a well-burped baby. Coroner says it was a heart attack. I had Viola put a notice on the door of his shop." Viola Fahrner was the newest deputy on the force, a slightly overweight black woman who had moved here from Indianapolis three years ago. Her job description was little more than that of a meter maid, but she showed promise.

"Yes, I see the notice. We're standing in front of the antiques store, me and the girls."

He knew that meant her fellow members of the Quilters Club. That foursome had been inseparable since high school. Even through college and close to forty years of marriage. "Come on over and have a cup of coffee," he invited. "Myrtle just made a fresh pot."

"Thanks, but we just had breakfast at Cozy Café. Maisie had watermelon waffles this morning."

"Is she still serving breakfast? I could go for watermelon waffles."

"Jim, your diet," his wife reminded him. They were both trying to loose weight. "You had a stack of pancakes before you left the house this morning."

"Yeah, well –" Jim Purdue was a broad, burly man with a balding head. He reminded you of the guy who played the brother-in-law in TV's "Breaking Bad." However, for a seasoned lawman he was remarkably kindhearted, more likely to give a hitchhiker five bucks than haul him in for vagrancy. "Did Maisie say what the lunch special was going to be? I'm getting together with Beau at noon."

"You'll be happy. Hot Dog with Pork and Beans." Van Camp's Pork and Beans was very popular around here, the recipe for beans in tomato sauce created in 1889 by the son of an Indianapolis grocer.

"Yum," he said. Looking at his watch.

~ ~ ~

Maddy no sooner got home to that stately Victorian mansion on Melon Pickers Row than she heard the phone ringing. Fumbling with her keys, she let herself in and raced to the kitchen, that wall phone being closest.

"Hello," she said, breathless from the race into the house. She didn't have caller ID, so the identity of the person at the other end of the line was a surprise.

"Mom, it's me – Bill," her son's voice filled her ear.

"Bill, is anything wrong?" It couldn't be N'yen, for he'd been living with her and Beau the past year. And Bill and Kathy were divorced, so it wouldn't be her. "Are you all right?"

"Everything's fine. Maybe more than fine. Kathy wants us to get back together."

"Oh? I thought she was teaching in Ohio."

"She only had a one-year contract. And that's up for renewal. But she wants to come home to Chicago."

"T-that's great," Maddy said.

"I thought we'd give it a try. See if it works out."

"And N'yen?"

"He'd best stay with you and Dad till we see if this second time around takes hold."

"That's probably a good idea," Maddy said. "We'll be rooting for you guys. Love you, hon."

When Madelyn Madison hung up the phone, she was surprised by her conflicting feelings. She certainly hoped things worked out for Bill and Kathy, but the thought of N'yen going back to his adoptive parents was like a dagger in her heart.

PART II

CHAPTER SEVEN
Greater Midwest Occult
Phenomena Association

MADDY MADISON COULDN'T HELP BUT GASP when she opened her front door and came face-to-face with Maury Seiderman. He was the weirdo who had once tried to steal the Mad Matilda Wilkins treasure. One of the Quilters Club's previous cases.

Seiderman had been distantly related to the old witch woman and wanted to claim his cut of her fortune. He did that by pulling a gun on Maddy and her friends. But Bootsie had smacked him with a shovel and called the police. The 6-foot-3 nutcase barely escaped going to jail.

"Ah, my good lady. Do you perchance remember me?" Seiderman gave her his crooked smile. He still sported a pencil-thin moustache like an old-time movie star, but his linear stretched-out stature and unusual purplish eyes made him look more like a space alien that was posing as human.

"Yes, Mr. Seiderman, I do remember you. Last time I saw you, you were threatening to shoot me."

"Forget the past. That was all a misunderstanding," he insisted. "No hard feelings, I hope."

"Exactly what are you doing here on my doorstep?" She was vaguely uncomfortable with his presence.

"I'm here in an official capacity, madam. As you may recall, I work as chief field investigator for the Greater Midwest Occult Phenomena Association.

We've had a report that you saw a flying saucer."

"An unidentified flying object," she corrected him. "I think it was actually sunlight reflecting off an airplane."

"People are often confused by what they see. Flying saucers are sometimes mistaken for birds, clouds, weather balloons, lightning and fireballs, you name it!"

"There was a airplane overhead," said Maddy. "I'm pretty sure that's what I saw."

"Do you mean that Cessna a body fell out of?"

"Oh, you've heard about that? Yes, that airplane."

"A terrible accident. Nonetheless, we have to check very carefully, be certain of what you saw. Aliens are all around us, you know."

Maddy silently counted to ten, at an impasse on whether to correct him that the death had not been an accident, or to challenge his assertion about little green men from outer space. Instead, she said, "If you have any questions, you'd best check with Police Chief Jim Purdue. He has my statement. And I'm told he just arrested the owner of that plane."

From the flicker in his strange eyes she could tell he remembered Chief Purdue, the lawman who had arrested him for brandishing an unlicensed firearm. You don't threaten the police chief's wife and her friends and get away with it. "No, that w-won't be necessary," he stammered. "Sorry to have taken up your time. I must get on to my next appointment."

She watched as Maury Seiderman briskly walked to the other side of the street where he'd parked his rental Nissan. As he settled behind the wheel and switched on the engine, she saw him position – what was it? – yes, an aluminum-foil hat on his head. To prevent aliens from reading his mind, no doubt.

What a whack job, Maddy thought as she eased the door shut and flipped the deadbolt to LOCK.

~ ~ ~

"Who was that?" asked Aggie. She and N'yen had been helping their Grammy bake a watermelon upside down cake. The aroma of a cake in the oven, the kitchen smelled like a holiday. Flour covered the counter like an unseasonal dusting of snow. N'yen has a white dab on his nose.

"Do you remember that crazy guy who tried to steal Mad Matilda's treasure? It was him, Maury Seiderman."

"The treasure that didn't exist?" sniggered N'yen. Everybody ended up empty handed. That had been a bit of a fiasco for the Quilters Club. No treasure, but they *did* solve a murder in the process.

"I remember that creepy guy," said Aggie. "He looked like a giant preying mantis. I think he has a few screws loose."

Maddy laughed. "Yes, I agree he has more loose screws than a Studebaker."

"A what?" asked the teenager.

"That's an old make of car," explained Mr. Brainiac. "The last Studebaker was built in 1966."

"I wasn't even born then," said Aggie. "Heck, that's even before my mother was born."

Maddy tried to stifle a smile. "Well, Miss Smarty Pants, I was only nine years old in 1966. As a matter of fact, my dad – my adoptive dad, that is – owned a '62 Studebaker Gran Turismo Hawk. A sporty red coupe, as I recall."

"Too bad you don't still have it," N'yen said matter of factly. "The GT Hawk is considered quite collectable. Half a century later about 900 of them are still on the road."

"How do you know these things?" asked Maddy, amazed at the boy's font of knowledge.

"I read," he said.

CHAPTER EIGHT
On the Lam

HORACE HAMMETT GREELEY – his associates called him Horace the Hammer – had gone to the mattress in Indianapolis. As a made man he knew he could count on Salvatore Milano to take care of him. The Indy mobster owned a rundown motel on the outskirts of the city that he used as a safe house when needed. Ensconced in Room 201 at Evergreen Inn, ol' Horace knew he was well hidden. He'd registered under the name Dick Tracy, his way of thumbing his nose at the cops.

Horace the Hammer hadn't minded helping the Boss get rid of a "loose end," that former bagman who had been subpoenaed to appear before the grand jury. No need to take any chance that this *pazzo gavone* might become a confidential witness. CWs were too high a risk.

Being a recreational pilot, Horace had bought himself a Cessna Turbo 172 Skyhawk JT-A, an expensive toy that he used to ferry friends to Vegas on gambling junkets. With his connections, the rooms and meals were always comped – a little perk that came with working for Salvatore Milano. And on a few occasions he'd flown Sal for clandestine meetings with associates in Chicago. Indy fell under the oversight of Joseph "Joe Fish" Alphonso, the *capo de tutti capi* who headed up the Chi-Town Outfit.

Technically, Horace was an enforcer, not a button

man. Rough people up – sure. Break a few legs – why not? But he didn't normally get asked to do wet work. Nevertheless, when Sal asked the favor, he didn't have the option of saying no.

Throwing that *goombah* out of the plane had been no big deal. The pigeon didn't even see it coming; a quick shove and he was flying like a bird.

All would have gone smoothly if some busybody hadn't seen the bagman take his dive. Horace had spotted the woman and her two kids as he circled back over the swamp. No doubt she'd seen the N-number on the side of his plane. That's why he'd dumped the Skyhawk for pennies on the dollar and turned lammest.

He would certainly miss that sweet ride.

~ ~ ~

Lou Ritchie had been released from police custody after providing the title that proved he'd purchased the Cessna Skyhawk two days *after* someone took a nosedive out of it. The paperwork showed he'd bought it from a Burpyville man named Horace Hammett Greeley.

A quick check with the Burpyville Police confirmed that Greeley was a minor mob figure. Even though he wasn't Italian, Salvatore Milano supposedly had taken a liking to the young thug. Good muscle was hard to find.

Police Chief Frank Crenshaw said Greeley had a reputation for roughing up people for the Indianapolis boys, but he'd never been charged with a crime. No vics would testify against him. Last year there had been a complaint that he buzzed the tower at Burpyville Regional Airport. He got a warning. That was all. A fairy clean rap sheet, as it turned out.

Nonetheless, he was on the lam. A check of his apartment in a complex on the Southside showed he'd skipped. Suitcase missing, several bureau drawers empty, shaving kit gone. Neighbors hadn't seen him since earlier in the week. The Burpyville Police put out an APB.

Chief Jim Purdue and Chief Crenshaw had known each other since high school. Matter of fact, Frank had dated Bootsie before she set her sights on Jim. Nevertheless, there was a high degree of cooperation between the neighboring police departments. For this one, a crime that stretched between the two jurisdictions, they agreed to set up a joint taskforce.

That afternoon Jim Purdue and one of his deputies drove over to Chief Crenshaw's office to kick off the collaboration. Deputy Evers Gochnauer had been assigned as liaison. With his boss nearing retirement, Gochnauer was angling for the top position. But the other deputy, Petie Hitzer, was strong competition. It would be a horserace.

The Burpyville Police Department was located on Jailhouse Street, but the old jailhouse had been torn down long ago and a new facility erected on the other side of town. Burpyville being ten times larger than Caruthers Corners, its PD occupied a two-story brick building that covered an entire block. Deputy Gochnauer parked his cruiser in the paved lot in back and followed Chief Purdue through the rear door that was used only by cops.

At the desk, Jim Purdue announced they were there for a conference with Chief Crenshaw. He was told they were expected.

The police station actually had a conference room, a luxury that Jim Purdue only dreamed of. As they walked into the depth of the building he passed a couple of interrogation rooms with one-way mirrors, a well-equipped forensics lab, a records department, and a small lunchroom well-stocked with coffee and donuts – but there was already a carafe of steaming hot coffee, Styrofoam cups, and a wide selection of Krispy Kremes waiting on the big conference table.

Evers Gochnauer was sure he'd died and gone to heaven. He took a seat within easy reach of the tray of donuts. Chief Purdue sat next to him. Frank Crenshaw and a couple of his men took the facing side of the table.

"How do you figure Horace the Hammer for this murder?" Chief Crenshaw opened the conversation.

"Horace the Hammer?"

"That's Horace Greeley's street name. Word is he uses a rubber mallet to break knees when Sal Milano wants to send a message to somebody in Burpyville. But we've never been able to catch him at it."

"Still, there's a number of crippled lowlifes around town," one of Crenshaw's deputies added with a barely suppressed grin. Bad guys get little sympathy from lawmen.

"How do we figure Horace Greeley for the murder?" Jim Purdue repeated the question. "One of the witnesses recognized the make of the plane. A door had been removed so we figured it was being used for skydiving. We called the nearest jump school and it turned out the owner had just bought the plane from your boy Horace." It sounded pretty simple – A + B + C – when Chief Purdue put it into words.

"Good policing," the other lawmen complimented him.

"Owe it all to that thirteen-year-old boy who recognized the make and model of the airplane."

"Sounds like a smart kid. Maybe he can help us figure out how to catch Horace the Hammer. I'd bet a dollar against a donut Horace is holed up somewhere within a fifty-mile radius of here."

"Caruthers Corners, you think?" asked Deputy Gochnauer.

"I was thinking Indy," said Chief Crenshaw. "Salvatore Milano can better take care of him there."

CHAPTER NINE
The New Proprietor

BEFORE MARK TIDEMORE became mayor, he'd been an attorney. When he came back home after a stint at a high-powered Los Angeles firm, he'd bought Bartholomew Dingley's practice when the old man retired. Being one of the town's few lawyers, Mark had drawn up Dan Sokolowski's Last Will & Testament.

As a World War II Holocaust survivor, Daniel Elisha Sokolowski had few living relatives. His Will named a distant cousin – Jakub Szymon Żuraw – as sole heir. It turned out that Żuraw had passed away last year at the age of 87, so the inheritance wound up going to his 28-year-old grandson, Kacper Antoni Żuraw. Born in America, the grandson had legally changed his name to Casper Anthony Crane – Żuraw meaning "crane" in Polish.

The name change made Crane difficult to locate, but a private detective turned him up as a 6th-grade schoolteacher in Cincinnati, Ohio. Given the size of Dan Sokolowski's estate (half a million dollars on deposit at Caruthers Corners Savings & Loan, plus the antiques shop), Casper had resigned his teaching position with Brandon P. Semple Middle School and relocated to Indiana to take over "the family business," as he called it.

Mark Tidemore didn't much like the young man. He displayed none of the warmth and goodwill ol' Dan had been known for. He quibbled over every penny in the estate, even complaining about the money paid to the private detective to find him. Mark donated his own fee, escaping some of the parsimonious nitpicking.

Mark, Beau, Jim, Edgar, Ben, and Freddie acted as Dan Sokolowski's pallbearers. Rev. Benjamin Durrenberger of the First Mennonite Church led the service, there being no rabbi in town. The closest synagogue was Temple Sholom over in Burpyville, but Dan had never been known to attend that particular *beyt knesset*.

In recognition of the deceased's heritage, Rev. Durrenberger asked mourners to say "*Baruch dayan ha'emet*," a blessing recognizing God's power as the true judge. He concluded with a recitation of "*Kel Maleh Rachamim*," a prayer of remembrance:

> "*Al molay rachamim, shochayn bam'romim, ham-tzay m'nucha n'chona al kanfay Hash'china, b'ma-alot k'doshim ut-horim k'zohar haraki-a mazhirim ...*"

> "God, full of mercy, who dwells on high, grant true rest upon the wings of the Divine Presence, in the exalted spheres of the holy and pure, who shine as the resplendence of the firmament ..."

Casper Crane stood there at graveside, wearing a black suit and weeping as if he'd been close to this cousin he'd never met. The signage on the antiques shop had already been changed to Crane's Antiquarian Attic. A notice in the window stated: Under New Management.

"Things will never be the same," sighed Agnes Tidemore.

She had been friendly with Daniel Sokolowski, hanging out at the dusty emporium, peppering him with hundred of questions about everything from Thomas Chippendale chairs to Limoges boxes to Wedgwood china.

"*Co moi noi cu,*" said N'yen. "That's an old Vietnamese saying. It means, 'New one in, old one out.' "

"Oh yeah, Benjamin Franklin said, 'Be slow in choosing a friend, slower in changing.' "

"What's that mean?"

"Be cautious before accepting Casper Crane as Daniel's replacement."

"You're awfully standoffish," he shrugged. "I'll stick to the advice of my ancestors."

"Aw, what does some old Buddhist monk know?"

"Don't make fun of my heritage, *my trang.*"

She kicked his ankle. "What did you just call me?"

"Ow. I called you a white American. What's wrong with that?"

"Nothing. It just sounds more like an insult in Vietnamese."

"I'll take the sayings of a monk over those of a fat kite-flying windbag."

She kicked his ankle again. "Don't you disparage *my* heritage."

"Ow," he said, hopping on one foot. "That hurt."

"Serves you right, you –"

But before she could complete her sentence, their grandmother leaned over and said, "*Shhhhh.* You're at a funeral."

~ ~ ~

After the services the pallbearers and their wives

and children gathered at Cozy Café for slices of freshly baked watermelon pie. In honor of Daniel Sokolowski, Maisie said it was on the house today.

Aggie and N'yen requested vanilla ice cream on their pie. The slices were so warm the ice cream quickly melted, filling the shallow plates with a thick white puddle that the kids dished up with a spoon.

"Manners, please," Maddy said to the two teens.

"Listen to your Grammy," Tilly Tidemore said to reinforce the message.

"Yes ma'am," Aggie responded rotely.

Always the know-it-all, N'yen said, "In Vietnam slurping is considered a compliment to the cook."

"Dear, we're not in Asia," winked Lizzie.

"No, we're at 40° North, 85° West," said the boy as if he had just consulted a world map.

"Well, uh, I guess you're right," sputtered the redhead, her cheeks matching her hair.

"N'yen, don't be rude," said Beau Madison."

That got the boy's attention. "Yes, Grampy. Sorry, Aunt Liz." His grandfather's approval mattered to him more than anything. Beauregard Hollingsworth Madison IV had become his role model.

"Did you catch the pilot who pushed that guy out of the airplane?" asked Ben Bentley, catching the police chief's eye.

"Not yet," Jim Purdue allowed. "We had to let the guy who now owns the Cessna go. But we got the name of the jasper he bought it from – Horace Greeley."

"You mean that newspaperman who said, 'Go West, young man'?" asked Aggie, looking baffled.

"Same name, different fellow," grinned her Uncle

Jim. "Problem is, he's disappeared. We haven't been able to find him anywhere, even with a six-state All Points Bulletin."

"You're saying Greeley sold his plane and got outta Dodge?" commented Mark Tidemore. As mayor, he was following this murder investigation closely.

"That's about the size of it," nodded the police chief.

"Ha! I'll bet the buyer – what's his name? – Upside Down Lou – got a darned good price," laughed Edgar Ridenour. As a former banker, he was always looking at the money angle.

"Yeah, he picked up a $450,000 airplane for $150,000," confirmed Jim Purdue. "It was practically new."

"Has the killer cashed the check?" asked Aggie, her logical mind zooming in on a potential lead.

"Didn't think of checking on that," admitted Jim Purdue, looking a little embarrassed.

"Out of the mouth of kids," said his wife, patting him on the forearm.

"Hey, I'm fifteen now," Aggie pointed out. "Mom is letting me date."

Everybody looked at Tilly. "Well, kinda," Aggie's mom admitted. "Mark has okayed her going out with Bobby Elwood, as long its either a party or a double date."

"Mostly Bobby and I go to the movies with Pricilla Moretz and her boyfriend Teddy DiMacchio. There's an AMC Multiplex with 8 screens in Burpyville."

"Aggie never invites me," N'yen complained.

"Don't worry, Best Buddy." Beau ruffled the boy's raven-black hair. "Soon enough you'll be double dating too."

"How can I? I don't even have a car," he sulked.

"What kind of car would you like?" asked Bootsie. She winked at Maddy to show she was being playful.

"A Batmobile."

Beau laughed. "That may be hard to come by. You may have to make do with borrowing the family Toyota."

"Could I have driving gloves?"

"Driving gloves?"

"I've always wanted driving gloves. Like Steve McQueen wore in that movie *Le Mans*."

"Hey, I've got a pair I'll give you," offered Jim Purdue. "Don't use 'em anymore." A few years back, Jim had bought a Mazda MX-5 Miata in response to an incipient midlife crisis. But he'd sold the sports car when one of his deputies stopped him on Highway 101 for speeding. Forthwith, he packed away his $150 Fratelli Orsini lambskin driving gloves, along with his 100% sheepskin Miata Motorsport jacket. Ah, the memories.

"Gee thanks, Uncle Jim. My own gloves!'"

"No biggie, Little Buddy. And when you get old enough, I'll teach you how to drive."

"Aww, that's three years away."

"Only two. In Indiana you can get a learner's permit at fifteen, That is, if you're enrolled in a driver's education course."

"Aggie's lucky. Being a girl she can get boys to drive her anywhere."

His cousin wagged a finger at him. "Bobby Elwood is my age; he doesn't have a license. Teddy DiMacchio drives us to the movies because he's dating Pricilla. Teddy's a year ahead of us in school, so he has a driver's license. And his own car, a Honda CR-V."

"Oh well, I get to go fishing with Grampy and Uncle Edgar. A boys-only outing."

"*Humph*, I've been meaning to talk with you about that," declared Aggie, transforming into full feminist mode. You might have thought she was preparing to burn her training bra. "Those fishing trips are discriminatory. Aren't girls allowed to fish?"

"Hey, I don't want to go fishing," Lizzie spoke up. "You could break a fingernail casting those lines."

"You can count me out too," laughed Cookie. "I don't like baiting hooks with wiggly ol' worms."

"Worms," said Aggie, making a face. "Would I have to do that?"

"'Fraid so," nodded her grandfather. Although he and Edgar mostly used chicken livers when fishing for catfish.

"Also, you have to take the catfish off the hook when you catch one," added N'yen. Knowing she didn't like to touch slimy things like muddy bottom fish. "They've got sharp whiskers so you gotta be careful not to let one cut you. That can hurt!"

"Ooo-ee," she frowned. "Maybe I don't want to go fishing after all. But it's still exclusionary to not even invite me."

"Come out with us next weekend," said Edgar Ridenour, going along with the flow of conversation. "I'll bait your hook for you."

"No thank you, Uncle Edgar. I think I'll stay here and work on my Amish Log Cabin quilt. Aunt Lizzie is going to help me add the batting."

CHAPTER TEN
Can't Get There From Here

CRACKLETON CROSSING is a wide place in the road north of town, little more than a scattering of rundown houses occupied by various members of the Crackleton clan. The community's matriarch was 98-year-old Sarah Celine Crackleton – known to everybody hereabouts as Granny. Most people agreed she was nuttier than a five-pound fruitcake.

Granny liked sitting on her front porch and talking with passersby. That's where she was when the Nissan Versa pulled up, the odd-looking guy with the purplish eyes leaning out the driver's window to ask directions.

"Which way to Gruesome Gorge State Park?" he inquired. Strangely, he was wearing a tin-foil hat on his head.

The old woman took a sip of Big Red Soda. The bottle promised that it was "Made With Real Sugar." Granny had a sweet tooth. "Can't get there from here," she said with a belch.

"Really, my good lady, you can get anywhere from anywhere. Just point me in the state park's direction."

"Hard to do."

The thin man stretched farther out the car window. Almost like that comic book character, Plastic Man. "This is a crossroads, my dear lady. There are only four choices, three if you subtract the direction I just came from."

"Why d' you want to go to Gruesome Gorge? It's just a big gash in the ground where a bunch of Indians got massacred. That was back in 1830 or -31, don't remember which. That was even before *I* was born."

Maury Seiderman was getting frustrated. He'd never been a man of patience. "I want to see where that woman spotted a flying saucer. I'm a field investigator with the Greater Midwest Occult Phenomena Association. G.M.O.P.A. for short."

"Flying saucer? What does that Maddy Madison know?" the old woman spat. "Can't seem to make up her mind. She now claims it was an airplane. That's what it said in yesterday's *Gazette*."

"I'm here to get the facts."

"I saw a space ship one time," Granny said, an aside. "It was a sight to behold."

"You don't say?"

Granny pointed with her chin. "It landed in that field over yonder," she indicated a grassy space across the street. "A li'l spaceman got out, walked over to the general store, and bought hisself a soda pop."

"A soda pop?"

"It was a bottle of Sprecher Root Beer, as I recall."

"Aliens like root beer?"

"They gotta drink something. It's a long way between planets."

By now, he was convinced the old woman was lying. Or crazy.

When she said, "The li'l fellow took me for a ride in his space ship. Went to Indy and back in less than ten minutes –" he opted for crazy.

Alien abductions were real, but flying saucers

were not some interplanetary Uber service.

~ ~ ~

Maury Seiderman took a right turn at the crossroads, just a guess, having failed to get directions from that loony old witch woman. That actually sent him on the right path, but then he'd turned onto Highway 21 at Buddy Flynn's Texaco, winding him back to Caruthers Corners. This expedition wasn't going well.

As he drove, he thought about Granny Crackleton's farfetched story of an alien visitor buying a bottle of root beer. That was hard to believe. Where would an alien get money to pay for a pop?

Caruthers Corners was small enough to drive through without noticing. The Main Street was only a few blocks long, not many storefronts at that. The town's center was a four-block grassy square with a bandstand, koi pond, and Ferris wheel. The residential neighborhoods spread out from there in a small grid of tree-lined streets.

Seiderman parked next to the Town Hall. The meters only required 25¢ an hour. Across the street was the Town Square. The bandstand would be a good place to meet his new patron, a local businessman who believed that the Truth Was Out There when it came to UFOs. A $10,000 donation had been bandied about in their earlier phone conversation. He'd have to remember to thank that woman at Cozy Café for the introduction. Maisie Walters had come up with a $1,000 herself.

This town was going to be a fundraising bonanza.

~ ~ ~

Maddy got another call from her son Bill. "Hi, Mom," he'd gushed. "Just wanted to report that things are going well between me and Kathy. We're talking about giving it another try. Isn't that great news?"

"Yes, dear. I'm happy for you and Kathy. You were always such a terrific couple."

"Thanks, Mom. Kathy and I *do* have so much in common. She wants to come back to work at the kids center. I could sure use the help."

Despite her words, Maddy was worried about her son and his ex-wife getting back together. They were both such idealists, their view of life not always realistic. They wanted to save a world that often didn't want to be saved. The couple was as close to being latter-day hippies as you could come without living in a commune. Their naiveté sometimes worked against them.

"Well, we're rooting for you two," she said, not sure if she really meant it.

When two people are so much alike, there's no counterbalance in their relationship, she told herself. That could prove to be problematic.

CHAPTER ELEVEN
Alien Grays

MAURY SEIDERMAN eyed the effete young man walking across the Town Square. The grass had been cut that morning and the dewy blades stuck to the visitor's wingtip shoes like confetti. The man was tall and thin, almost a mirror image of Maury Seiderman. But where Maury's eyes were an unnatural lavender, this fellow's eyes were as dark and lifeless as lumps of coal. And where Maury wore tattered thrift-store chic, this guy could have stepped out of an Abercrombie & Fitch catalog.

"Casper Crane, I presume," said the UFO investigator, standing to greet him. Seiderman had been sitting on the bandstand steps, watching kids line up for rides on the nearby Ferris wheel. A colorful new fixture for the Town Square. At 10¢ a ride, it was a bargain.

Crane was still wearing the black suit he'd selected for his cousin's funeral. That and his solemn expression made him look more like an undertaker than a newly minted antiques dealer. He held out his hand in greeting, more of a formal gesture than a friendly salutation. "You're the flying saucer nut?"

The description took Seiderman aback. This was not the attitude he would have expected from a potential patron. The woman at Cozy Café had said this guy was interested in making a $10,000 donation to G.M.O.P.A. In fact, the guy had confirmed it earlier, when they had arranged this meeting by phone.

"I'm a senior executive with the Greater Midwest Occult Phenomena Association," he carefully reminded the man. "We're a non-profit research group out of Chicago. We investigate reports of Unidentified Flying Objects."

"Do you actually believe in that crap?"

"Yes, of course," he replied. "Don't you?"

~ ~ ~

Fact was, Maury Seiderman *did* believe in flying saucers, but not in little green men. He knew that aliens were a different color.

As founder of the Greater Midwest Occult Phenomena Association, Maury had familiarized himself with all the statistics: 43% of all reported alien encounters describe them as being humanoids with smooth gray-colored skin, large hairless heads, dark almond-shaped eyes, slits for mouths, and no ears. The number of fingers was in dispute.

Grays, they were called in ufological circles.

Ufology is the study of UFOs.

The term Unidentified Flying Object was coined back in 1953 by the United States Air Force to cover the myriad of flying saucer reports they were receiving. The shorter acronym of UFO was first used by Captain Edward J. Ruppelt, the director who headed Project Blue Book, the USAF's official investigation of Unidentified Flying Objects that ran from 1952 to 1970.

Project Blue Book defined a UFO as "any airborne object which by performance, aerodynamic characteristics, or unusual features, does not conform to any presently known aircraft or missile type, or which cannot be positively identified as a familiar object."

While UFO sightings go back in history – including the Biblical story of a fiery chariot in Ezekiel 1:4-28 – the euphemism "flying saucer" came about in 1947 when pilot Kenneth Arnold spotted five disc-like objects flying in formation near Mount Rainier in Washington State. He estimated their speed at 1,200 mph. Arnold described them as looking like "a pie plate" or like "a saucer skipped across water." The saucer description stuck.

However, the United States Air Force listed Arnold's sighting as a mirage.

Project Blue Book concluded that "(1) no UFO reported, investigated, and evaluated by the Air Force has ever given any indication of threat to our national security; (2) there has been no evidence submitted to or discovered by the Air Force that sightings categorized as 'unidentified' represent technological developments or principles beyond the range of present-day scientific knowledge; and (3) there has been no evidence indicating that sightings categorized as 'unidentified' are extraterrestrial vehicles."

Most studies found that the majority of UFO sightings are misidentified conventional objects or natural phenomena.

A cover-up, some claimed. Maury Seiderman's Greater Midwest Occult Phenomena Association among them.

~ ~ ~

"As I told you over the phone," repeated Casper

Crane, "I'm willing to contribute $10,000 toward your cause."

Seiderman was confused. "Why would you do that if you think our research is crap?" There, he'd said it.

"Clearly, I want something in return," said Dan Sokolowski's distant cousin. "I'd be pretty stupid to give you that much money and not get something for it, right?"

"R-r-r-ight," Seiderman answered slowly, purplish eyes not blinking.

"Good," the antiques dealer offered a thin-lipped smile. "I'm glad we're on the same page."

"And exactly what do you want in return for your contribution?" May as well get to the point.

"I want you to kill someone."

"W-what?" stammered Maury Seiderman. He involuntarily took a step backward, trying to distance himself from the madman. What was this talk about killing someone? He'd thought he was meeting with a potential supporter. A donor. Fighting aliens took money.

His heel came up against the edge of the bandstand. Losing his footing, Seiderman tripped over the high wooden step. He felt his ankle snap, the bone broken he was sure. His back hit the risers with the force of a prizefighter doing down for the count. His head smacked hard against the plank flooring.

"Owwwwwww," he moaned with intense pain. "Call 9-1-1." He knew he was going to need an ambulance.

CHAPTER TWELVE
Amish Quilts

THE LATE DAN SOKOLOWSKI had always stocked a good selection of handmade Amish quilts. His customers appreciated the variety. Typical designs included Heart of Roses, Center Diamond, Sunshine and Shadow, Log Cabin, Jacob's Ladder, Tumbling Blocks, Bear Paw, Garden Maze, and Double Wedding Ring. The workmanship on Amish quilts was "exquisite," to use Lizzie Ridenour's description.

Although many people are familiar with the Old World lifestyle of the Amish, few truly understand their beliefs and tenets of faith. The Amish are in fact Christians — they believe in Jesus and in the Holy Trinity.

While the Amish share the belief of most Protestants that salvation is an unearned gift from God, they reject the belief that anyone can be certain that his salvation is guaranteed. They consider such certainty to be arrogant.

Known for their horse-and-buggy lifestyle, the Amish choose to live separately from the world and modern technology. That includes foregoing electricity, that being viewed as a connection to the outside word. Amish homes are recognizable by the lack of electric lines.

The Amish reject any civilian authority that contradicts their beliefs. They accept no public funds, don't participate in Social Security, do their own schooling up to 8th grade, and avoid joining the military.

They follow the Ordnung, an oral set of rules that govern every aspect of Amish life. This code of conduct has evolved over decades, differing slightly from one Amish congregation to another.

There are 50 Swiss Amish church districts surrounding Caruthers Corners. Founded by Swiss settlers in the mid-1800s, this is the Hoosier State's second-largest Amish community.

That's why Dan's Den of Antiquity stocked a wide selection of quilts. The inventory record showed 22 in all. Lizzie Ridenour had agreed to purchase all the quilts for the Hoople Quilting Heritage Museum. She had been given a $10,000 grant for the acquisition by Maddy's new trust fund.

The transaction had been handled by Dan Sokolowski's cousin, the 28-year-old twerp who had taken over the antiques shop. Casper Crane had decided to focus on furniture and high-end works of art, narrowing the inventory considerably from the hodgepodge ol' Dan had stocked. Always willing to help his neighbors, Sokolowski sometimes had acted more like a pawnbroker than an antiquarian. Unredeemed goods accounted for two *Kwakwa̱ka̱'wakw* totem poles, miscellaneous farm tools, children's toys, and even a pogo stick.

Dan's cousin intended to class up the business. No more pawning of items, no quilts, no collectibles, nothing newer than World War II. All prices were immediately doubled. Free coffee was suspended.

Enough of this lackadaisical approach to business. Making money required disciple, he told himself.

~ ~ ~

Aggie was feeling sad over the loss of her friend, Mr. Sokolowski. She would miss visiting him in his dusty old antiques store and peppering him with questions about his various merchandise. He had lots of odd things on display.

One of her favorites was a first edition of *The Adventures of Sherlock Holmes* by Arthur Conan Doyle, an 1892 First Edition published by George Newnes, London. Bound in the original publisher's gray cloth with bright gold lettering on the boards, this was a true first edition without the name on the street sign and "Violent" for "Violet" on page 317. What's more, it was signed on the flyleaf by the author himself.

Being a member of the Quilters Club, Aggie considered herself to be a detective (amateur status), for she had helped her Grammy and friends solve several important cases here in Caruthers Corners. Owning a First Edition of *The Adventures of Sherlock Holmes* would be a great homage to her idol, Mr. Sherlock Holmes. Oh, she knew he was a made-up character, but that didn't stop her admiration of his keen logical mind and how he solved *The Sign of the Four* and other cases. She'd had to make do with a used Reader's Digest Reprint Edition, but that was better than nothing.

She'd enjoyed browsing about Dan's Den of Antiquity, making new discoveries with each turn of the corner. Other objects which had caught her eye included a chunk of the Berlin Wall (she'd read about it in school); a Knights Templar sword with an intricately etched blade; a sealed jug of water from the Fountain of Youth in St. Augustine; a cookie jar that looked like Buddha; a faded tin button that pictured *Mad*'s Alfred E. Neuman with the caption "What, Me Worry?" underneath his gap-toothed countenance; a nickel-plated Colt .45 revolver said to have belonged to Bat Masterson; a bottle of brownish liquid labeled "Love Potion No. 9"; and a ventriloquist's doll that looked like the Monopoly Man, complete with a monocle and top hat.

She wondered if Daniel Sokolowski's cousin would be nice like him. Would he let her daydream as she wandered the labyrinth of antiques and oddities in the shop? This being Saturday, N'yen was off fishing with Grampy and Uncle Edgar. Leaving her behind as usual – what did you have to say about that, Ms. Gloria Steinem?

Oh well, maybe she and Tige would wander down to – what was its new name? – Crane's Antiquities Attic and introduce herself to the new owner.

CHAPTER THIRTEEN
Paramedics on Call

THE FIRE DEPARTMENT'S PARAMEDICS carried Maury Seiderman to Burpyville Memorial's Outpatient Clinic. A sprained ankle didn't need the hospital's ER unit.

The injured man kept insisting it was broken, but X-rays didn't show any fractured bones. The docs bandaged him up, gave him a bottle of pain pills, and subjected him to a thorough physical examination to make sure there were no other injuries. None turned up, other than a bruised ego.

He'd been embarrassed by the crowd that gathered around him in the Town Square as he lay there next to the bandstand, moaning like a baby. That guy Casper Crane had disappeared, obviously not wanting to be seen with Maury.

Kill someone – was Crane insane?

Just because he'd once been charged with brandishing an unlicensed firearm at the police chief's wife didn't mean he was a murderer for hire. His crimes had been more in the nature of swindles and scams.

Now he lay here on a hospital gurney, being poked and prodded, examined from head to toe. His hospital gown didn't close in the back, so when they made him stand up (on one foot) to be weighed, the nurses could see his tushy. It was very humiliating.

Maury Seiderman insisted on being issued crutches. How else was he to move around with his ankle disabled and his spinal column badly bruised? A physical therapist fitted him up with a nice aluminum pair, fully covered by his insurance policy. The Greater Midwest Occult Phenomena Association had good employee benefits. He'd seen to that when he set up the one-man company.

~ ~ ~

As Aggie headed to Crane's Antiquarian Attic, she noted some sort of hubbub going on in the park across from her home. She and her parents and her two baby sisters lived in the old Taylor Mansion, the same house her Grammy had grown up in. It faced the Town Square. She didn't even have to leave her porch to hear the bands playing in the gazebo-like bandstand on summer nights and watch the windmill-like churning of the neon-lighted Ferris wheel.

Standing there on the gingerbread-covered porch, she spotted a paramedic truck backed up to the curb on the other side of the Square. It looked like someone was being loaded into the back. She wondered if her Uncle Freddie was involved. As the town's fire chief, the paramedics reported to him. He sometimes made runs with them, just to keep his skills sharp. Last month he'd helped save Miss Emily Polk's life when she suffered a heart attack. It was hard for Aggie to believe Miss Emily – that odd duck who lived out at Wabash Acres – was her great, great, great aunt on her Grammy's side. The sister of the woman who had given her Grammy up for adoption.

Turned out, Grammy had been the secret "love child" of Emily's sister Sue Ann and Herbie Hoople. So had Maisie Walters. That's how they came to inherit that big pile of money from the Hoople Quadruplets Trust Fund.

How could you bring yourself to give your baby away to another family? she wondered. N'yen was adopted, but that was because his mom and dad had died in a car wreck. And her cousin Donna Sue was adopted, but her mom had died in an apartment fire.

Aggie guessed her dog was adopted too. She'd picked Tige out of a cardboard box marked "Give this puppy a good home." And she'd given the little fellow a *very* good home. He got fed Alpo and table scraps and old soup bones. Plus he was allowed to sleep at the foot of her bed.

Tige trotted behind her as she made her way along the backside of the Town Square, past the circular Ferris wheel and past the stately bronze statue of ol' Ferdinand Jinks, keeping well out of the way of the paramedics. She couldn't make out who they had on the gurney, but it looked like they had his leg wrapped in a soft splint. Had he fallen off the Ferris wheel perhaps?

As Aggie passed Cozy Café she waved to Maisie Walters through the big plate-glass window and the waitress waved back. That was hard getting used to too, the idea that Maisie was her Grammy's twin sister. Separated at birth, as the saying goes. But Grammy and Maisie Walters didn't look anything alike. Maybe they should send their DNA off to Ancesters.com and get tested, just to be sure there had been no mistake. Just as babies could be separated at birth, she'd read about crib mix-ups where people took the wrong newborn home. Maybe Grammy's True Twin was living nearby, unaware that she had a sister ... just like Grammy didn't know she was really a Hoople instead of a Taylor until a year or so ago.

Tige ignored Mrs. Warton's cat. Alexander the Great was perched atop the trashcans behind the diner. He hissed a greeting – or warning – to the wire-haired dog.

Aggie didn't stop at the DQ, planning to do that on the way home. She had just enough of her allowance left to buy a Chocolate Blizzard with sprinkles. She wouldn't be needing any money tonight because Bobby Elwood always paid her way to the movies. They would be double-dating with Prissy and Teddy. A new Marvel superhero movie was playing at the Multiplex. It seemed like there was *always* a new Marvel superhero movie playing at the Multiplex.

Pausing in front of the antiques shop, she looked up at the new sign: Crane's Antiquities Attic. That was kind of silly, she thought. This wide storefront was ground level, not an attic at the top of a house. Poetic license, she supposed. But she had preferred the wordplay of Dan's Den of Antiquity. If she didn't become a private eye when she grew up, she might become a writer. Or maybe she'd compose verses for greeting cards. Or do TV jingles. At fifteen, she had plenty of time to make up her mind.

When Aggie pushed on the door to enter the antiques shop, it didn't bulge. That's when she noticed the sign on the door, a round cardboard clock face displaying the message: Back in One Hour.

How was Mr. Sokolowski's cousin going to make a go of this place if he didn't keep regular hours? She was irked that she had walked all way to this end of Main Street for naught. Then, a smile edging at her lips, she turned and walked back to the DQ to buy herself a Blizzard.

CHAPTER FOURTEEN
Visitors from Outer Space

THE TOWN COUNCIL MEETING had ended and everybody was sitting around the long conference table swapping gossip, local news, crop reports, and speculation about the weather. Typical of the monthly sessions. Town business didn't take much time, Caruthers Corners being a small municipality with not a lot of business to discuss.

Conversation covered these topics:

- The weather was warm. The summer, mild.

- The Colts had a great starting quarterback in Jacoby Brissett, but nobody could top five-time MVP Payton Manning.

- Two new businesses were moving into the town's industrial park, a sock looping company (High Top Hosiery, Inc.) and the distribution center for an online novelty company (JoyBuzzer.com).

- The passing of Daniel Sokolowski. He'd been on the Town Council. Everybody liked him.

- The hunt for the pilot in the skydiver murder. No progress there, reported the Police Chief. The FAA was still looking for the airplane.

"At first Maddy thought it was a UFO," offered Beau Madison. "She was staring into the sun. But then she saw the body tumble out."

"I once saw a flying saucer," interjected Karl Schaeffer. Fat Karl was a new member on the town council. He worked as assistant manager at the Wal-Mart in Burpyville, but he lived up near Never Ending Swamp.

"You mean a UFO," corrected Chief Purdue.

"No, flying saucer. It was silver and round like a pie plate. I could see it plain as day."

"Just when was that?" asked Mark Tidemore. The mayor was being polite to the council newcomer.

"Last year," Fat Karl recalled. "Saw it hovering over the treetops behind my house."

"Sure it wasn't swamp gas?" challenged Edgar Ridenour. He'd seen plenty of that while fishing along the Wabash.

"Or maybe St. Elmo's Fire," suggested Bobby Ray Purdue. One of the richest people in Caruthers Corners, the police chief's cousin had been added to the Town Council a couple of years ago. He had backed the local petting zoo.

"No, a flying saucer. I know what I seen," insisted Fat Karl. Weighing in at close to 300 pounds, Karl had won the watermelon-eating contest at the annual Watermelon Days Festival several years in a row. Something of a legend among eating contest contenders.

"I believe you," chimed in Boyd Aitkens. "My daddy was a fighter pilot during World War Two. He was with the 415th Special Operations Squadron. He used to tell stories about round glowing objects chasing their planes on night flights. Those lights could fly rings 'round them, he said. The term 'flying saucer' hadn't caught on yet. My daddy and his buddies called 'em 'Foo Fighters.'"

"I've heard of them," nodded Big-Nose Evans, also a new council member. "Foo Fighters. There was a rock band named after them World War Two UFOs."

"That guy Horace Greeley wasn't flying a Foo fighter or a flying saucer," said Chief Jim Purdue. "He was flying a Cessna 172 Skyhawk."

"Did Greeley ever cash that check Lou Ritchie gave him for the airplane?" asked Beau.

"Yeah, the very next day. Probably did it on his way out of town. Took it all in cash. The bank had to scramble to come up with $150,000. Burpyville Federal doesn't usually keep that much on hand."

"Did the bank record the serial numbers?"

"Unfortunately not. Frank Crenshaw – the police chief in Burpyville – says they got flustered and didn't do that."

"So it's a dead end?" asked Mark Tidemore.

"As dead as that skydiver."

CHAPTER FIFTEEN
Intrepid Treasurer Hunters

"WELL, ARE YOU GOING to tell us?" nudged Cookie Bentley. The Quilters Club had gathered at the Hoople Quilting Heritage Museum for its weekly confab. The large table in the sewing room was strewn with fat quarters and fabric scraps. Patterns and needles and spools of thread lay everywhere. Partially completed quilts were draped over wooden racks. Dog-eared copies of *Quilters World*, *American Patchwork & Quilting*, *Addicted to Scraps*, and *Quick Quilts Magazine* were scattered about the room.

A visitor might have mistaken it as the site of a bomb blast.

Maddy Madison looked up from her stitching. "Tell you what?" she asked. Playing innocent.

"You know, about the Jinks gold."

"You're asking *me*?" Maddy laughed. "Cookie Bentley, you're the one who gave me the clue about how to figure out its location."

"Me? I haven't got an inkling where to look."

"C'mon, Maddy," said Lizzie Ridenour. "Everybody thought it was at the old Jinks homeplace. That's what the inscription on the sons' rings said: *The foundation of my home is golden*. Clear proof that old man Jinks buried his gold there."

"That's right," nodded Bootsie Purdue. "And those crazy Crackleton boys spent years digging around the old building looking for the treasure. Even killing

83

people to protect it. What more proof did we need?"

"But it *wasn't* there," Aggie pointed out. The voice of reason.

"True," admitted Cookie. Always swayed by facts.

"Thank goodness, those evil miscreants are doing jail time," said Maddy. "They murdered Beau's brother." The three Crackleton brothers – Dub, El, and Vis – were each doing a 45-year sentence at Indiana State Prison. No chance of parole.

"Poor Uncle Mycroft," said N'yen in a sad voice. He'd only met the man a few times, but the boy was very bonded to his new family.

~ ~ ~

Nguye n Văn N'yen was born in Chicago's St. Anthony Hospital in 2004. His parents, Nguye n Quang Dung and Tran Thi Khiem, had left Vietnam in the spring of 1975, part of the exodus initiated by the fall of Saigon. By the time Thi Khiem gave birth, she was fairly old for motherhood. Having just turned 50, she had to resort to in vitro fertilization using the eggs of a younger woman. That was problematic for a good Catholic couple but they had all but given up hope of having a child.

N'yen was a precocious child. His parents entered him in Avery Coonley, a school for academically gifted students in Downers Grove. An IQ score of at least 124 is required for admission. N'yen had no trouble being accepted. Even at 3 he was performing at a sixth grade level.

Despite the distance, the boy's parents drove him from the Back of the Yards neighborhood where they lived to ACS each day, then picked him up in the afternoon. They did not mind this hardship. As the Vietnamese saying goes, *"Dau xuôi duôi lot."* The rough translation: A good beginning makes a good ending.

Nguye n Quang Dung owned a successful bakery in southwest Chicago. He was famous for *banh chuoi nu o ng*, a delicious banana cake baked in a pan to give it a crisp golden-brown exterior. This was a traditional Vietnamese dessert. He had an excellent kitchen staff, which allowed him and his wife the flexibility to drive their son back and forth to school. Although a day school, ACS did not provide bus service.

Four years later, returning to the bakery after having dropped N'yen off at school, Nguye n Quang Dũng's old Nissan Sentra was hit by a Wal-Mart truck on the Stevenson Expressway. I-55 was crowded that morning and the Wal-Mart guy had tried to pass a line of cars. Both Nguye n Quang Dũng and Trin Th☐Khiêm were killed in the head-on collision.

With no other relative than his Uncle Võ in Cleveland, N'yen was put up for adoption. At nine, he met his new parents – Bill and Kathy Madison.

CHAPTER SIXTEEN
Worth Killing For

LIKE HIS AVIARIUM NAMESAKE, Casper Crane was tall and gawky. His legs seemed abnormally long for his body. But he was still several inches shorter than that flying saucer freak, Maury Seiderman. What had he been thinking, trying to hire that weirdo to whack that Quilters Club lady?

Not that Crane had changed his mind on murdering her. He simply realized he'd picked the wrong guy to do the job. That Seiderman fellow had two left feet, not to mention a few marbles missing. He'd be more likely to shoot himself than that Ridenour woman.

Back to the drawing board. There had to be a killer-for-hire in, say, Indianapolis. Maybe he should put a coded ad in Craig's List?

He'd heard you could find such services on the Dark Web. But Casper had been a 6th-grade schoolteacher. What did he know about accessing these hidden reaches of the Internet where assassins and gunrunners and drug dealers lurked?

With his lanky, awkward appearance, the students at Brandon P. Semple Middle School had called him Ichabod behind his back, a reference to the Washington Irving character who ran from the Headless Horseman. His own cowardice had been documented in front of his class when the school's assistant principal had fired him in front of everybody and he'd just slinked away with his head down. Losing his job had been the real reason he'd decided to move to Indiana and take over his late cousin's antiques shop.

Problem was, he didn't know a Chippendale from a chipped teacup. That's how he'd inadvertently sold off that valuable Map Quilt. He never would've known its value if he hadn't stumbled across ol' Daniel's journal while cleaning out that oak roll-top desk in the backroom.

Now he had to get it back. He'd inherited a nice bundle from this relative he'd never met, but the quilt was key to millions in hidden gold. Yes, millions. That was worth killing for.

~ ~ ~

Maury Seiderman was panicky. The idea that Casper Crane wanted him to murder someone was preposterous. He might be a small-time grifter, but he certainly wasn't a hitman-for-hire.

He wanted to get as far away from this Crane guy as possible. Being he was at the Burpyville hospital he decided to go in the other direction, hole up somewhere in Indianapolis and let his ankle mend. Then he'd figure out what to do next.

The rental car company agreed to swap cars for him, picking up the blue Nissan Versa in Caruthers Corners and issuing him a green Toyota Corolla, delivered to the hospital door. That was the nice thing – the pickup and delivery – about a customer-friendly Empire Rent A Car franchise in a small town.

The Toyota had automatic transmission, of course. That meant Seiderman could drive since it was his left foot out of whack. He stacked his aluminum crutches on the passenger side. Heading to Indianapolis, he'd pick up a change of underwear and a shaving kit at some easy-access Dollar General store on the way.

Two hours later, Maury Seiderman was checking into a motel that he'd picked at random, a seedy place on the outskirts of Indy called Evergreen Inn. At $49 a night, he could afford to stay here until his ankle was feeling better.

~ ~ ~

The motel didn't have a restaurant or offer room service, but Maury Seiderman could order pizza delivered from a joint across the street. Luigi's Italian Take-Out advertised "2 Pies for $10." Maury liked pizza. And if he got tired of that, the menu included calzones, meatball subs, and hot buffalo wings. A virtual smorgasbord of greasy indigestible food. But it would do.

Not that he was eating that much. The painkillers he'd been given by the doctors really worked, zonking him out for hours at a time. Maybe he was taking too many, but his damned ankle hurt. Maybe it *was* broken. It wouldn't be the first time a physician had misdiagnosed a patient, he told himself.

But they had taken X-rays and given him the works. In fact, the experience had been quite humiliating. Treating him like a slab of meat. Sticking him with needles designed for horses. Probing him. Parading him around with his ass showing out the back of that gown. It made him angry. Really angry.

Or maybe that was just the painkillers talking.

~ ~ ~

The FBI listed the Chicago-based G.M.O.P.A. as "a benign organization made up of hobbyists. At last count there were 32 members. Maurice Gilbert Seiderman, its founder, is the only employee. Seiderman is considered mentally unstable. He has a long record of petty criminal offences, mostly swindles and confidence games. He is not viewed as a threat."

However, the Feebies might have reconsidered their evaluation if they had known about Maury Seiderman's latest scheme. High on pain pills, he was planning to blow up Burpyville Memorial's Outpatient Clinic. Somehow, Seiderman had come to believe it was a secret headquarters for Grays.

He had mistaken a routine prostate examine for an Alien Anal Probe.

PART III

CHAPTER SEVENTEEN
The Wrong Homeplace

AS EVERY SCHOOLCHILD in Caruthers Corners knew, the town had been founded in 1829 by a wagon train of hardy pioneers led by Jacob Abernathy Caruthers, Ferdinand Aloysius Jinks, and Col. Beauregard Hollingsworth Madison. A broken wheel had stranded them here on the banks of the Wabash River. That was back when the area was still known as Indian Territory – long before the name Indiana came into use. The Potawatomi who lived in these parts did not welcome the interlopers. Fierce battles ensued, with the musket-toting settlers eventually winning out.

Today, there's only one Native American to be found in Caruthers Corners, a 25-year-old night watchman at the Industrial Park named Metea Davis. He had grown up on a reservation in Oklahoma, but returned to the home of his people in search of his heritage. He found little.

Potawatomi call themselves *Neshnabé*, meaning "Original People." They were here long before the white settlers.

The History of the Indian Territory, 1800 - 1900 by Nelson Lawrence Chadwick tells the story. However, most of what we know about the founding of Caruthers Corners comes from *A History of Caruthers Corners and Surrounding Environs*, a thick book written by Martin J. Caruthers. The author claimed he got the stories from his grandfather, Jacob Abernathy

93

Caruthers himself.

There was nothing in Martin's book about missing gold. Nonetheless, local legend had it that Ferdinand Jinks brought a wagonload of gold with him from Massachusetts, where he'd been a wealthy merchant.

Ol' Ferdie had given each of his three sons a ring that offered a clue to where he buried it. Or at least that was the theory Maddy Madison and her Quilters Club pals had come up with.

Daniel Sokolowski had helped them figure it out, but recent excavations around the Jinks homeplace turned up nothing. Those crazy Crackleton boys had been digging there for years in search of the treasure without luck.

The clue had been the inscription on the circumference of those rings: *The foundation of my home is golden.* They had figured that meant the Jinks gold was buried at the family home, now little more than a ramshackle structure barely defying the laws of gravity.

"We were right," Maddy insisted. "We just picked the wrong homeplace."

~ ~ ~

Turns out, Cookie Bentley had unknowingly helped Maddy figure it out by citing from the history books. According to Martin J. Caruthers' tome, Ferdinand Aloysius Jinks had "settled on the banks of the Wabash" after the wagon train broke down in 1829. But the Jinks homeplace where everybody had been digging was more than a mile from the muddy river.

"There must have been an earlier house," Maddy reasoned. "And that's where ol' Ferdinand buried his treasure."

"I seem to remember hearing that there were remains of an old house built by one of the Founding Fathers near the river," mused Lizzie. She and Edgar lived on a hill overlooking the Wabash, their home a Midwestern version of Scarlett's Tara. Pretty fancy by local standards. They knew their neighborhood well, owning one of the few residences on River Road.

"Maybe we'll have to search along the river," Maddy speculated. Almost as if talking to herself.

"Oh boy, a field trip," said N'yen, laying aside his iPad. The boy was weary of sitting around the house with a gaggle of females. The platter of watermelon cookies was empty, save for a few crumbs.

Aggie sniggered. "You're just tired of losing that stupid game to Beelzebub666."

"I'm not losing," the boy said. "I'm just luring him into a false sense of confidence. It's a strategic move."

"Right."

"And the game's not stupid," he said petulantly.

"This is going to take some searching my files," Cookie decided.

"The information must be pretty obscure if *you* can't remember it," Bootsie said, acknowledging her friend's super memory.

"Yeah, well –"

The group accompanied Cookie back to her office at the Perricock Museum of Science & History. The Caruthers Corners Historical Society occupied a wing of the big stone monolith that overlooked the town. Docents watched over the exhibits in Cookie's absence. There had been a steady stream of visitors since the

Historical Society put the Madison Meteorite on display.

"Back here," Cookie led them to the file room. As Executive Director, she was one of the few people who had access to this inner sanctum, but she breezed past her assistant with the Quilters Club following her like a gaggle of goslings.

"Do you think there's a record of Ferdie Jinks's first house here in Indiana?" asked Bootsie.

"There must be," said Lizzie. "After all, there was that reference in *A History of Caruthers Corners and Surrounding Environs*."

"Let's not be overly optimistic," warned Cookie. "Martin J. Caruthers is not exactly known for accuracy. That history book was written mainly to aggrandize his ancestor, Jacob Abernathy Caruthers."

"Let's hope he's right about Ferdinand Jinks's first home," said Maddy. "Or else my theory of where he buried his gold is kaput."

"True," said Cookie. "But I'm not sure where to look for that first house." That wasn't good news. With Cookie's forget-me-not memory, she of all people would remember any references to Ferdinand Jinks's first house in Indiana.

"How about land records?" suggested Bootsie.

Cookie shook her head. "Land records don't go back to 1829," she said.

"Newspaper articles?"

"There were no papers back then."

"Deeds?"

"They burned up in the Great Conflagration of 1899," the blonde woman said, pushing her glasses higher on the bridge of her nose. This was getting frustrating.

"Old letters?"

"The Society doesn't have any Jinks family correspondence."

"Martin J. Caruthers' research papers?"

Cookie sighed. "We have some of his notes, but I'm not sure he did any real research. He claimed he got the stories from his grandfather."

All the while she had been thumbing through the file cabinets, checking this folder and that. Not finding anything helpful.

"Why not ask Mr. Aitkens?" Aggie spoke up. "My Daddy says Boyd Aitkens owns most of that land along the river. Maybe he knows where the original Jinks place was."

Everybody turned and stared at the girl.

"Can't hurt," Cookie said.

CHAPTER EIGHTEEN
The Watermelon King

AITKENS PRODUCE WAS THE LARGEST watermelon grower hereabouts. Boyd Aitkens secretly underwrote the annual Watermelon Days festival, knowing it was good publicity for his money crop. He belonged to the Illiana Watermelon Association, the organization of watermelon growers, shippers and other industry supporters in the bi-state area (Illinois and Indiana).

According to the Register of Deeds, Boyd Aitkens owned 23% of all the land in Caruthers County. He had accumulated old family farms and undeveloped acreage and raw countryside, converting most of it into productive farmland. In addition, he owned a small vineyard, two housing subdivisions, grazing pastures for cattle, and some scrubland along the Wabash River.

His humongous six-bedroom ranch house was flanked by assorted barns and outbuildings as well as a metal warehouse larger than an airplane hangar. Long semitrailers were parked off to the side; closer in were the tractors and pickups; in front of the main house were several Cadillacs and Mercedes. A widower with one living son, he had built quite a financial empire. He served on the Town Council, acted as adviser to a couple of the governor's committees on agriculture, and sat on several boards. He had done well for a local boy whose father had been a tenant farmer.

A big balding man with a handlebar moustache

(that was new), he greeted his visitors with warmth. He had grown fond of the Quilters Club and heartily supported their sleuthing. They had helped find the murderer of his son Charlie. His other son Ralph had dated Maddy's daughter Tilly in high school, before she'd hooked up with Mark Tidemore.

"Hi there, girls. What brings you out this way?" He lived seventeen miles outside town, about midway between Never Ending Swamp and the river.

Naturally assertive, Maddy took the lead. "Hello, Boyd. We thought you might help us locate a historic site – Ferdinand Jinks's first home when he came here in 1829. We think it may be on your property along the Wabash."

"Ferdinand Jinks had a house on the river? Don't think I've ever heard that," the man replied, rubbing his chin as if trying to stoke up a memory. "No, doesn't ring a bell."

Bootsie's shoulders slumped with the news; Lizzie let out a disappointed sigh; Cookie just said "Drat!" But Maddy plowed on determinedly. "Are you sure about that? There was a mention of it in Martin J. Caruthers' history book."

"The former mayor's father was a blowhard. I knew him well. My father used to tend land for him. You shouldn't believe a single word he wrote in that book without two corroborating sources. Those pompous Caruthers are out to glorify old Jacob Caruthers as Town Founder, like Jinks and Madison didn't exist."

As head of the Historical Society, Cookie Bentley knew the genealogy charts. Boyd Aitkens wasn't descended from any of the Founding Fathers, his forbearers arriving fifty years later. His gripe was with Martin J. Caruthers himself, once a major land baron in these parts who worked tenant farmers like slaves. Boyd's dad had been one of them and the boy never forgot his family's mistreatment at the hands of Martin Caruthers.

In an unexpected turnabout, the Caruthers clan lost most of their holdings during the '70s due to bad investments in vermiculture and Boyd Aitken became wealthy by buying up cheap land and converting it to watermelon fields. Much of that land had originally belonged to ol' Martin.

To this day there was no love lost between the Caruthers and Aitkens kinfolk.

But that didn't mean Boyd Aitkens was wrong about the loose facts in *A History of Caruthers Corners and Surrounding Environs*. While it was the best record available, Cookie knew to take it with more than a grain of salt. A five-pound bag might be more appropriate.

"So you're saying Ferdinand Jinks never had a house near the river?" pressed Lizzie. Today she was dressed in red. Along with her faming hair, she looked like a study in scarlet.

Aitkens took off his hat and rubbed the sweat off his receding forehead with a big yellow handkerchief. "No, I'm just saying if there were one, I don't know about it."

"My husband Edgar said he's heard something about an abandoned Jinks homestead down the river from where we live," Lizzie continued.

"There are lots of abandoned homesteads along the

river. Early settlers didn't know the Wabash floods every now and again. We're sitting on a flood plain. In 2011 the Wabash River rose nearly 24 feet – the highest water level since 1943."

"The Flood of 1913 was even higher," Cookie pointed out. Her eidetic memory on display.

Boyd Aitkens shrugged. "So a lot of early structures were abandoned as people moved to higher ground."

"Thank goodness my house is on a hillside," said Lizzie Ridenour. "In 2011 the water got halfway up our yard."

"Guess we're just wasting our time," frowned Bootsie Purdue. "We'll never know for sure if Ferdinand Jinks had a house on the river before he built the one next to the Madison farm." Even though the lands now belonged to Boyd Aitkens, local folk still referred to the parcels as "the old Jinks place" and "the Madison farm."

"One person who might could help you," Aitkens raised the possibility. "That's Granny Crackleton."

"That old witch," snorted Maddy derisively. She was unforgiving that the Crackleton boys killed her husband's brother and threatened her and the children.

Thank God they were serving 45-year sentences in the state prison with no chance of parole anytime soon.

"She's the oldest person in the county," the watermelon farmer reminded her. "And she's a Jinks by birth."

"True," said Bootsie. "But Granny Crackleton would never tell us anything. She thinks the Jinks gold belongs to her."

"The Jinks gold!" exclaimed Boyd Aitkens. "Is that what this is about? Well, ladies, let me be clear about it. If there's any gold found on my land it belongs to me."

~ ~ ~

"No way I'm going to go ask Granny Crackleton about where Ferdinand Jinks built his first house here in Indiana," declared Lizzie Ridenour. "She would see right through it." Lizzie was the only one of the group who'd ever had a conversation with the old woman. Aggie had been there too, but being a teenager she didn't count.

"If Granny thought we were looking for the gold she might send her son Jeb to kill us all," worried Maddy. She didn't trust the Crackleton family. They were both crazy and dangerous – a bad combination.

"Do you really think so?" asked Lizzie, easily rattled.

"One of those Crackleton boys killed Beau's brother," said Maddy. "Don't forget that."

"I still think we need to talk with Granny," insisted Cookie.

"Don't look at me," replied Bootsie. "That old woman wouldn't let the police chief's wife in her door without a warrant."

"Well then, I guess that leaves me," grumbled Cookie. "I'll tell her the Historical Society is trying to pinpoint lost landmarks, hoping to get them listed on the National Historic Register."

"Think that will work?" asked Maddy.

"Who knows?" shrugged Cookie. "Maybe she'd like to see her ancestor's original homeplace honored on the Historic Registry."

"Yes, but that sense of pride could be outweighed by the risk of having people poking around where the treasure's buried," Bootsie argued.

"But Granny doesn't know that the treasure's buried there," Aggie reminded them. Being levelheaded as usual. "Remember, the Crackletons still think it's buried at the other Jinks house – where they were digging."

N'yen wasn't convinced. "Problem is, if we remind her about the original homeplace she might realize her mistake."

"Hmm, good point," admitted his grandmother. "So what do we do? Give up?"

"No way," Aggie reasoned. "If we give up, nothing happens. So if she refuses to help us, we're no worse off."

~ ~ ~

While the Quilters Club was planning this assault on Crackleton Crossing, Maury Seiderman answered a knock at his motel door. His pizza, no doubt.

"That the pepperoni with sausage?" he asked, digging into his wallet for a $20 bill. He'd been to the ATM in the lobby earlier that afternoon.

The chubby boy in the T-shirt that said "2 Pies for $10" looked at the ticket. "No, this is pepperoni with olives," he said. "My mistake, this is meant for Room 201. You're in 202."

"Where's *my* pizza?"

"I'll have to go back and get it. Won't take long. We guarantee delivery within a half hour or your money back."

"Half hour!" exclaimed Seiderman. "Luigi's is just across the street. I can see it from here."

"Yeah, so? I got other pizzas to deliver."

"But I ordered first."

"Tough toogies."

"Hey, don't get smart with me. I'm going to complain to your manager."

"Go ahead. My dad owns the place. I work for free, so he ain't gonna fire me."

The delivery boy knocked on the next door. 201 swung open cautiously and a man with a broad face and heavy brows peeked out. "Yeah?" he growled.

"Your pizza. $5 plus tax."

"Good deal." He handed the boy seven ones and said, "Keep the change."

As the delivery boy departed, Maury Seiderman called after him, "Hurry up with my pizza!"

"What was that about?" asked the neighbor.

Maury Seiderman said, "The jerk mixed up our orders. I sent him back to get mine."

"Yeah? You want a slice of mine in the meantime," offered the guy in 201."

"Naw, I don't like olives. They make me hiccup."

"Never heard of that before," the guy said.

"My name's Maury. What's yours?"

"Hor– uh, Hammer."

"Like that movie star Armie Hammer?"

"Uh-uh. Like the rapper MC Hammer."

"Oh. I don't know much about rap music."

Horace the Hammer took a bite from his pizza. "What're you doing here in Sal's motel?" he asked. He didn't recognize this beanpole with odd purplish eyes and a pencil-thin mustache. Maybe he was a new recruit.

"Who's Sal?"

"The owner."

"Oh." Maury Seiderman was feeling woozy. The pain pills. "I'm hiding out," he mumbled.

His neighbor laughed. "Ain't we all?"

"You see, a man asked me to kill someone. I don't do that sort of thing."

Horace the Hammer smiled. "Maybe I can help you out on that."

CHAPTER NINETEEN
Granny Crackleton's Visitor

GRANNY CRACKLETON HEARD THE CAR pull up out front, but she didn't recognize the bespectacled woman with dishwater blonde hair who knocked on her door. "Come on in,' Granny called, mainly because she didn't want to stand up and go to the door. Her arthritis had been acting up.

"Mrs. Crackleton —?"

"Call me Granny. Everybody does."

"I'm Katherine Bentley. But call me Cookie. Everybody does."

"Well, Cookie, what can an old crone like me do for you? You need a potion to help your love life?"

"No, my husband and I are doing just fine. I came to see you because I'm the director of the Caruthers Corners Historical Society."

"That a fact? Didn't I read in the *Gazette* that your outfit moved up to the Perricock Mansion?"

"That's right. The Society recently moved into a wing of the Perricock Museum of Science & History. We're the history part."

"And you want me to tell you some history stories? About when I was a young girl during the Great Depression? Don't remember much about Herbert Hoover, but I once met Franklin Delano Roosevelt. I was a 12-year-old girl at the time. He came through here campaigning for the Presidency. But he didn't get out of his big touring car. Just sat there in the backseat waving at everybody."

"Something like that," said Cookie. "I'm trying to find about some of the old homeplaces around here. There might be some historic structures that need to be preserved. Some might deserve to be listed on the National Historic Registry."

"My, my. A bunch of tumbledown houses having historical significance. Who woulda thought?"

"What can you tell me about the house Jacob Caruthers built when he decided to settle here?"

"Everybody knows Jacob Caruthers sold his big fancy mansion to Abner Purdue – who turned it into the E Z Seat chair factory. Not much of the original structure left after all the additions and refitting. A real shame."

"How about Beauregard Madison's house?"

"You can find it still standing on what used to be the Madison farm. Boyd Aitkens owns the land now."

"And the Jinks homeplace?"

"It's all but falling down. On the parcel next to the Madison farm. Boyd Aitkens owns it too. He owns most of the land in the county."

"Didn't Ferdinand Jinks have an earlier home on the river?"

"Don't know as that'd count. He didn't live in it. Got flooded out before his family had a chance to move in."

"Where was it?"

The old woman paused to think. "I'm not rightly sure. Somewhere near Hairy Toad Bend, I recall my father said. Never been over there myself."

"And what about the Beasley Mansion ...?" Cookie

continued on, asking about this house and that. Trying to disguise her interest in the original Jinks house with a dozen other inquiries.

Granny Crackleton enjoyed being the "expert." She served Cookie elderberry tea and biscuits slathered with watermelon jam. The old woman wished her visitor had been able to stay longer.

~ ~ ~

"I can't believe you pulled it off, Aunt Cookie," said N'yen. "That was a swell piece of acting."

"Acting?" responded Cookie Bentley. "I *am* the executive director of the Historical Society."

"You did good," said Maddy, patting her on the hand. Even though this wasn't Tuesday, the Quilters Club had convened in the sewing room at the Hoople Quilting Heritage Museum to get Cookie's report.

"Talking with Granny Crackleton was actually interesting," admitted Cookie, looking around the room at her friends. "Granny's a chatty old soul. I learned a couple of new details about the early houses here in Caruthers County. Did you know Jesse James and his brother Frank spent the night at the home of Junior Jinks in 1869?"

"Junior Jinks?" said Bootsie, not as knowledgeable on local genealogy as her pal Cookie.

"Ferdinand Jinks's oldest son, Ferdinand Jr. He would have been in his 40s at the time. He was known to be a rapscallion. It's said he associated with bandits and bank robbers. Some say he rode with the James-Younger gang, but Granny Crackleton denied it. Didn't want to admit her uncle was a bank robber, I suspect."

Maddy looked up from her sewing. "She said the

James brothers spent the night at Junior's house?"

"Yes. They were on their way to a bank in Ohio, according to Granny."

"Where was Junior's house?" Lizzie asked. She had been showing Aggie how to use a Luixin Newman quilting thimble. It allowed one to quilt for hours without any pain.

"Over near the river. Granny said it was close to his father's first house. Up the hill from it, out of the flood area."

"But where?" asked Lizzie. Living on the river, she knew the area better than her friends.

"Near a spot called Hairy Toad Bend."

"Never heard of it," said Lizzie.

"Me neither," said Maddy.

"Make that three," added Bootsie, looking puzzled.

"Hey, I know where that is." N'yen looked up from his electronic game. Beelzebub666 was beating him again. He wasn't used to losing. It made him pouty. "Grampy and Uncle Edgar took me fishing there. Didn't catch anything."

"Let's go there right now," said Aggie. "Obviously that's where the gold is hidden."

"Hold on," said her grandmother. "Let's not get ahead of ourselves. We'd need shovels and stuff to dig for treasure."

"We don't have to dig yet," said the girl. "We can just scout it out."

"That's not a bad idea," nodded Bootsie. Always game.

Lizzie turned to the boy. "Do you think you can find this Hairy Toad Bend?"

"Sure."

"Okay," shrugged Maddy. "Put away your quilting supplies and let's go."

CHAPTER TWENTY
Hammer and Nailer

BEAU MET JIM PURDUE for lunch at Cozy Café, a weekly tradition held over from Beau's stint as the town's mayor. By all accounts, he had been a good mayor, but his son-in-law was turning out to be an even better civic leader. Because Caruthers Corners was such a small municipality, the mayor also functioned as the town manager. And under Mark Tidemore's steady guidance many new industries had come to the area. The population was growing little by little, reversing the past decade's steady decline.

Chief Purdue ordered today's special, the Hot Dog with Pork and Bean's. Beau had a fried pork tenderloin, an Indiana favorite. Coffee refills were always free at the café. Maisie was generous that way. A sign behind the counter promised:

FRESHLY MADE
MAXWELL HOUSE COFFEE
ENJOY A NEVER-ENDING CUP
ONLY 50¢

No "last drop" at Cozy Café.

The Police Chief sipped his coffee with a frown. He was frustrated over the lack of progress in locating his "person of interest" in what the *Burpyville Gazette* was calling The Skydiver Murder.

Catchy phrases sold newspapers.

And put pressure on local law enforcement.

The *Gazette*'s ace reporter Ralph Wrightson had

been on top of this bizarre murder like stink on a skunk. The two police chiefs were feeling the heat. CNN and The New York Times might be branded as fake news; but Indiana farmers and small-town merchants took their hometown papers as gospel.

"I can't help but feel this Horace the Hammer is hiding under our very noses," Jim said between spoonfuls of pork and beans. While an 1832 cookbook called *The American Frugal Housewife* contained a recipe for the bean dish, it wasn't until 1894 that the son of Indianapolis canner Gilbert Van Camp added ketchup to give his lunch snack more flavor. That was the beginning of what would become the Van Camp brand's biggest product line.

"Horace the Hammer?" Beau said.

"That's his street name."

"I'm sure his mother is very proud." The sarcasm obvious.

"Trust me, Horace Greeley's a very bad dude. Nothing like that old-time newspaperman who told people to go West. This particular Greeley works for an Indianapolis mobster."

Beau shrugged. "That being the case, I'd look for Greeley in Indy," he said, taking another bite from his sandwich. He chewed it slowly and deliberately, as was his personality.

"Chief Crenshaw is handling that end of it. Burpyville being closer to the state capital than we are, Frank has a stronger working relationship with the cops there."

"You have good ties to that FBI guy – what do you call him? – Neil the Nailer."

"Neil Wannamaker. He owes me a few favors."

"Why not get the FBI looking for your perp? The Nailer versus the Hammer."

Chief Purdue laughed, almost choking on his beans. "That's a good one. Hammer and Nailer. But the FBI doesn't have jurisdiction."

"Check with Mark on that – he used to be a lawyer, y' know – but I'd bet the Feds have dibs on crimes committed on an aircraft."

The police chief turned serious. "You think so? That didn't occur to me. I've never dealt with a murder that took place in the sky before."

~ ~ ~

Mark Tidemore knew the exact statute – Classification 164: Crime Aboard Aircraft.

"This is a 1961 law that made air piracy, interference with flight crews, and other acts aboard airplanes, such as murder, into federal crimes," he explained.

"Bingo," said Beau Madison. He was proud of his daughter's husband. Mark the Shark – as his courtroom opponents used to call him – had a sharp legal mind.

Chief Purdue was not entirely pleased. He just realized that the Feebies might be able to take this case away from him and his Burpyville counterpart. "Maybe we should think about this. I'd hate to see Neil Wannamaker walk away with this one."

"You and that FBI Special Agent in Charge are too competitive," chided Mark Tidemore, slipping back into his mayoral role. As such, he was the police chief's boss.

"Yeah, but –"

"Call him. Better you invite him in before he decides to insert himself whether you like it or not."

"Okay, if you say so," grumbled Jim Purdue. Not happy with his lack of choice.

"Look, jurisdiction is tricky here. You could have US Marshals, Homeland Security, Indiana State Police, the FCC, even the Airline Pilots Association trying to muscle into this murder investigation. Better you choose your partner. If the FBI gets involved, the others may hold off. And face it, you have a much better relationship with Special Agent Neil Wannamaker than you do with any of those other outfits."

CHAPTER TWENTY-ONE
Casper's New Partners

CASPER CRANE WAS SURPRISED when the bell over the door of Crane's Antiquarian Attic tinkled. He hadn't had any customers all day. Here it was 3:15 and he was thinking of closing up and going next door to the DQ for a Mint Blizzard. He had a taste for mint.

To his astonishment, that weird flying saucer guy hobbled into his shop. An aluminum crutch supported his bandaged left ankle. He hadn't seen him since that meeting a few days ago in the Town Square, when he'd tried to hire him for a little job. Now here he was again with some muscle-bound thug in tow. What was this about?

"Hiya, Mr. Crane," the tall gangly man greeted him. "Remember me, Maury Seiderman?"

"Sure. How's your foot?" He glanced down at the man's injured limb.

"Mending, but too slowly for my liking."

Crane got to the point. "What can I do for you, Maury? I'm sure this isn't a social visit." He was apprehensive this *schmuck* was going to try to put the squeeze on him over their brief conversation in the Town Square. It had been a mistake to approach him, but that woman who ran Cozy Café had described him as "shady." And he'd been looking for somebody with a questionable past.

"That business proposition you made —" Seiderman began.

"What about it?" Casper Crane said defensively, glancing nervously at the bruiser behind the skinny man. He was sure they were here to put the squeeze on him. Luckily, the police department was only a few doors away. He could call out for help if things got out of hand with Maury and his strong-arm guy.

"I'm outta commission with this bum foot, but if you still want some help my friend Horace here's willing to take on the assignment. But it will cost $15, not $10."

That got Crane's attention. "Horace, huh? You ever done this kinda thing?"

"Kill somebody? Sure, I'm the one what pushed Slick Eddy Williams outta that plane a few weeks back."

"No kidding?" Crane was impressed ... and a little frightened. "The cops are looking for you, y'know."

"They couldn't find a farmer in a haystack," laughed Horace the Hammer. "I'm not worried. Besides, I got powerful friends."

"That so?"

"Ask around in Indy, you'll get the word. So whattaya need done?"

Crane hesitated for a moment, then blurted, "Look, I need someone silenced. And a particular item retrieved."

Horace looked confused. "Is this a robbery or a whack?"

"Both. There's this busybody lady in town who has something I want back. And I don't need her telling people about it."

Maury Seiderman's purplish eyes seemed to glimmer. "Then this item you want retrieved must be very valuable. Its return might be worth more than $15 grand."

Casper Crane's head snapped up, face reflecting anger. "Hey, don't try to jack me up. I offered you $10,000 and that's still the deal."

"Yeah, but you're not in a bargaining position. How'd you like it to get back to the local cops that you're soliciting a murder?"

Crane stood his ground. "And how'd you like it if I told them you're harboring a criminal." He nodded toward the beefy man at Seiderman's side.

Horace the Hammer stepped forward, holding up his hands in a T like a referee might do. "Hold on, time out. You boys let this get out of hand, I'll have to whack you both. I'd hate to do that for free, but I've got my own butt to take care of here."

The air seemed to go out of both men. Crane and Seiderman looked at Horace as if just realizing he was there. And who he was – a killer on the run from the law.

"You're right," said Casper Crane. "No need to let this get out of hand." He could feel sweat trickling down the small of his back. "I think we can work something out."

~ ~ ~

Granny Crackleton told her son Jeb about the visit from the nice lady with the Historical Society. A willowy giant, at 6-foot-11 he made most basketball players look small. He had to stoop to pass through a normal doorway. A glandular problem, the doctors said. But he knew he was a genetic freak.

Aside from being a usurious loan shark, Jeb

Crackleton ran the convenience store across the street, a small emporium that gouged local folk on prices. But most people hereabouts were relatives. Known for extra fingers and other freakish mutations, the clan was said to be inbred. Birth records proved inconclusive for identifying parentage, in that the Crackletons relied more on midwives than hospitals. Much of the recordkeeping was questionable. Parentage was often fuzzy.

"You told her what?" Jeb shouted, clearly unhappy.

Granny had to tilt her head upward to address her elongated son. It gave her a crick in the neck. She could see the frown on his face. "Just stories like I tell the travelers who stop to chat with me on my front porch," she said defensively. "Nothing important."

"You said she was asking about old homeplaces."

"Uh-huh. She wanted to hear about the old houses that are still standing. And about the one that have tumbled down. Had a few questions about where some old ruins are located."

"Like what?"

"She had some idea about Ferdinand Jinks building his first house on the banks of the Wabash. I've heard the story, but I don't think he ever lived there."

"First house?"

"The river flooded. Drove Ferdie and his family out before they could unpack. So nobody ever claimed that place as home."

"But if they did, that would mean your grandpaw's house next to the Madison farm wasn't the home he was referring to on that ring you keep in a cigar box on your nightstand. It says *The foundation of my home is golden*. That'd mean we've been digging all these years in the wrong place."

"My daddy inherited the house on Old Patch Road. That's always been considered the family homeplace."

"But if Ferdie had a house before that, one he built when first settling here, that's where he would've buried the gold."

"I s'pose that's possible. But all his boys – my daddy included – thought the rings he gave 'em meant the gold was buried under our house on Old Patch Road."

"Your daddy and his siblings were congenital idiots. Old Ferdie's second wife was his brother's daughter. Your daddy Stanton and your Uncle Ace were missing a few marbles."

"Ferdie's oldest son was by his first wife. No problem there."

"True, but Junior never married. Never had any kids."

"Neither did Ace. He got hit by that Madison Meteorite when he was a young man barely grown."

"That means the scrambled brains came down through your daddy to you, you batty old witch."

"Don't talk to your mama that way. What brains you got, you got from me."

"What I got from you was this genetic anomaly that makes me seven feet tall."

"Oh, quit carping. You're only 6-foot-11."

"And look at my son Dub. A dwarf."

"Dub's serving hard time at the state penitentiary.

Forget that li'l worm."

"What about the twins? You know El and Vis ain't right in the head. Couldn't even kill the right man, those idiots."

"All three of them boys are on you. You married your first cousin on your daddy's side."

"How come Fatty Johnson turned out okay?" groused the giant. "He's got Jinks blood in 'em."

"Fatty's my baby sister's boy. The bad blood skipped them."

"Ain't fair."

"What are you complaining about, boy? You're richer than Croesus. You make more loans than the Caruthers Corners Savings and Loan. Practically everybody in the county owes you money. What d'you need with the Jinks gold."

"Don't matter whether I need it or not. That gold's my birthright. I deserve some compensation for being born into this crazy family."

"Ha! You're just greedy. Ain't enough gold in the world to make you happy."

"The Jinks gold would. But we've spent nearly forty years digging in the wrong spot, thanks to you, you stupid old woman."

"Who would've thought to look at them ruins down by the Wabash?"

"How come you never told me about that first house ol' Ferdie built?"

"Never thought much about it. Right after he built that li'l house, the Wabash overflowed its banks and flooded him out. That's why Junior built up the hill on that tiny parcel of land his daddy gave him."

"How do I find these ruins?"

"Never been over there myself. But it's at a crook in the river known as Hairy Toad Bend."

"I think know where that is. I'd better get over there 'fore your Historical Society lady starts poking around. She's friends with Beau Madison's wife. No telling what them Quilters Club biddies might come up with."

CHAPTER TWENTY-TWO
A New Task Force

POLICE CHIEF JIM PURDUE stood in the doorway of the Mayor's Office, fidgeting from foot-to-foot like a kid who needs to pee. Mark Tidemore looked up from the papers scattered on his desk and said, "What's up, Jim?"

"Just heard from the FBI. They pegged the fingerprints of our skydiver without a parachute. A two-bit punk named Edward Benjamin Williams. Known in Indy underworld circles as Slick Eddy."

"Did he work for Salvatore Milano?" Everybody knew who headed up the mob in Indianapolis, although Sal the Whisperer had never done a single day behind bars.

"Yeah, he was a bagman. Picked up winnings from floating crap games, according to Special Agent in Charge Neil Wannamaker. Slick Eddy was scheduled to testify before the Grand Jury. Guess Sal didn't like the idea that he might roll over on him."

Salvatore Milano was feared for his ironfisted rule over Circle City's mob scene. Many an errant gangster had disappeared without a trace. If it hadn't been for Maddy Madison thinking she saw a flying saucer, nobody would have found the body of Slick Eddy Williams in the midst of Never Ending Swamp.

The Boss was known as Sal the Whisperer because of his barely audible way of talking. Some said it came from a bad case of tonsillitis as a child. Others said it was an affectation to intimidate people, forcing them to stain to hear his words. And still others said it was to make it difficult for FBI wiretaps and hidden microphones to record conversations with his *capos*.

"So we know the vic," nodded the Mayor. As a former lawyer, he was used to police terms, like "vics" and "perps" and "persons of interest."

"We do, not that that helps much. We still can't lay our hands on Horace Greeley, the grifter who owned that Cessna 172 Skyhawk that Slick Eddy took the dive from."

"Isn't the FBI looking for him? You'd think they would have his picture on every Post Office wall by now."

The Police Chief removed his cap to rub his balding head. "Don't know about Post Offices, but Neil assures me they are turning over every rock from here to Chicago looking for Greeley. They even offered Sal Milano not to look too close into Slick Eddy's demise if he'd give up Horace Greeley. But no go. Sal takes care of his own."

"Why don't you ask the Quilters Club if they can figure out how to find this guy Greeley?"

Jim Purdue looked as if he'd just swallowed a prune. "Aw, gee, do you think they're smarter than the FBI?" The Police Chief was on delicate ground here, for he was talking about the Mayor's mother-in-law as well as his own wife and the wives of several Town Council members. Talk about being caught between a rock and several hard places.

"Can't hurt. They don't have to put themselves in harm's way. Just reason out where we might find the miscreant."

"In addition to my men and the Burpyville police, we've got the 35,104 employees of the Federal Bureau of Investigation on the case. What can four middle-aged busybodies and a couple of kids add to the party, except getting in the way."

Mark Tidemore laughed. "You better not let Bootsie hear you calling her a 'middle-aged busybody.'"

"I call her a busybody all the time," replied Jim Purdue with a weak smile. "Middle-age is a bit trickier ground to plow."

"Go ahead and ask the gals," urged the Mayor. "I suspect your life will be a lot easier if you do. Besides, I doubt you can keep them from doing it on their own."

"Yeah, there's that," mumbled the Police Chief.

~ ~ ~

N'yen was pleased with the news that his mom and dad were getting back together. But he was concerned over what that might mean. He'd been happy here in Caruthers Corners. He enjoyed hanging with his cousin Aggie. And he liked helping the Quilters Club solve crimes. After one case, Uncle Jim had given the boy a badge, making him an honorary deputy. It was shiny and gold-plated, just like the ones Petie Hitzer and Evers Gochnauer wore on their starchy blue uniforms.

Aggie cried when she heard the news. She tried to hide it, but he saw the tears before she turned her back and fiddled with the Log Cabin quilt she was working on. She didn't like the idea of her cousin going back to Chicago.

The members of the Quilters Club promised to throw him a going-away party, watermelon cake and all.

CHAPTER TWENTY-THREE
Hairy Toad Bend

MADDY'S BIG TOYOTA SEQUOIA bumped along River Road, the narrow cracked-asphalt roadway that follows the curve of the Wabash River for 37 miles on the western end of Caruthers County. N'yen sat in the front seat, acting as navigator for his Grammy. The remaining Quilters Clubbers were seated in the rear, but the roomy SUV was plenty comfortable for all. Even Tige.

"Just up ahead," said the boy, pointing through the windshield at a bend in the road.

"Oh my, are you sure this is right?" asked Maddy. Rounding the curve they came upon the riverside cottage that had belonged to Herbert Hoople, one of the famed Hoople Quadruplets. And Maddy's biological father.

"Pretty sure," said N'yen. "You can double-check with Grampy or Uncle Edgar. We fished for catfish in that cove across the river from that little house."

Everybody leaned forward to study the abandoned structure. No one had lived there since Herbie Hoople died a few years ago. The cottage's ownership had reverted back to the Hoople Quadruplets Trust Fund.

"Is this the Jinks homestead?" asked Bootsie, confused.

"No," said Lizzie. "Herbie Hoople lived here. The Jinks homeplace must be nearby. Edgar and I built our house three or four miles up the road. But we never pass by here. We get to our place by the entrance off Highway 101."

"So where's the Jinks place?" asked Maddy, pulling to the side of the road.

All swiveled their heads back and forth like patrons at a tennis match, surveying the bushy landscape. Nothing in sight.

"There's another house near here," N'yen told them. "You can see it from the river. It's up that way." He pointed up the hill. "Maybe if you drive another hundred feet down the road ...?"

Maddy eased her foot down on the accelerator, moving the Toyota forward at a snail's pace.

Nothing.

"I don't see anything," whined Lizzie.

"Me either," echoed Bootsie.

"Hold on," said fifteen-year-old Aggie, tapping on her iPhone. "I've pulled up a Google map of this area. Let me zoom in closer."

"It's up there, I tell you," insisted N'yen. Nose pressed against the passenger window. His breath produced a little circle of fog against the glass.

"Here it is," exclaimed Aggie, unable to hide her excitement. "You can see the roof up that way. And it looks like there's a driveway a little ahead."

"But that's not the house we're looking for," Cookie interjected. "That's the one built by Ferdinand Jinks's son Junior. We're looking for his father's first home, the one he built right after the wagon train broke down."

"Do you see anything else on that Google map?" asked Maddy, turning to look over the seat at her granddaughter. "Another house or ruins or the square shape of a foundation?"

"No," she murmured. "Just trees and bushes and the river."

"Look between Junior's house and the bend in the river," suggested Cookie. "Anything there?"

"Huh-uh."

In the front seat, N'yen pulled the iPad out of his backpack. "Let me try something. I have a link to the image database of the Ikonos-2 satellite. It might give us a better result than Google Maps."

"Why would it be any better?" asked Lizzie. Skeptical.

"Ikonos was the world's first high-resolution commercially-available satellite with imagery exceeding 1-meter resolution. It was launched into space in 1999 from Vandenberg Air Force Base. Ikonos is a 3-axis stabilized spacecraft, featuring 82-centimeter panchromatic and 3.28-m 4-band multispectral resolution – blue, green, red and near-infrared – which produces a false-color image."

"So what?" said Lizzie. Not very tech savvy.

"This high-resolution satellite imaging detects variations in the color of plant life around ruins," he explained. "It's been a great tool for archeologists."

"Huh?" Lizzie still didn't get it.

"I'm confused too," said Bootsie.

"He's saying this particular satellite takes a more detailed picture than Google's," Aggie interpreted.

"Not just more detail," corrected N'yen. "Its ability to manipulate color makes things stand out that might not be visible to the naked eye."

A muddy brown satellite image appeared on his

iPad. He tinkered with the toggles to reposition it, zoom in on this portion of Indiana, then enlarge it until the picture looked like the view from a low-flying plane. He touched another toggle and the image began to glow with strange, surreal colors.

"There," he said. "You can see the bend in the river, the roof of the Hoople Cottage, and over here is Junior Jinks's house."

The four women bent over the proffered iPad screen, emitting *ooh*'s and *ahh*'s.

"Do you see any sign of ruins?" prodded the boy's grandmother.

"Hmm, not offhand."

"But this *has* to be the right location," declared Cookie, scanning the screen with a laser-like gaze. "Granny Crackleton confirmed that her grandfather built his first house on Hairy Toad Bend."

"And she said it was near Junior Jinks's house, right?" said Bootsie.

"Yes, so this *has* to be the place."

"Could it be the Hoople Cottage?"

"I don't think so," said Maddy. Speaking with the authority of being a Hoople heir. "There must be ruins around here somewhere."

"Give me a minute to flip through the different color screens on this Ikonos photo," muttered N'yen, concentrating on the iPad screen. "There, no. There, no. There, ah, maybe this is something. The infrared screen."

"What?"

"Look right here," the boy pointed. "See those lines?"

Maddy squinted. "Looks like an L."

"Right, the corner of a foundation."

"Where's the rest of it?" asked Lizzie. The redhead liked everything to be plain and simple.

N'yen shrugged. "Maybe it's gone, washed away by the floods. Or maybe it just doesn't show up in this picture."

Cookie was looking out the car window. "Where would that be – down there in that flat area by the water?"

The boy looked from the screen to the river and back again. "I'd say yes."

Bootsie opened the car door and stepped out, Nike Dualtone Racers firmly planted on the blacktop. "C'mon," she coaxed her pals. "Let's go down there and check it out."

Lizzie slid out behind her, delicately extricating herself in a way not to muss her hair. She'd had it done just yesterday at the Helen of Troy Spa and Beauty Salon in Burpyville. "Do I need to take off my heels?" she asked, eying the mushy ground down by the water.

"Are those Jimmy Choos?" asked Maddy. "If so, I'd say yes." The Jimmy Choo Anouk patent leather pumps had cost $600 if they cost a penny. They would sink into the soft ground like spikes.

Lizzie put on hand on the Toyota's roof to balance herself as she struggled to remove them. "I don't know about this," she groused.

Cookie pushed out behind her. "You stay up here, dear. We'll go check it out." She, like the other two, was wearing rubber-soled Nikes, swoosh showing on their nylon sides.

Maddy and N'yen had already abandoned the front seat and were scrambling down the slope toward the flat area at river's edge. "Race you," grinned the Vietnamese boy.

"Slow down," called Maddy. "Your Grammy's not as nimble as she used to be."

"Hey," shouted Aggie, "wait for me." Giving up on her aunties to move out of her way, she exited the right-side door and circled the big blue SUV.

By the time the others (minus Lizzie) got to the flat area, N'yen was scratching at the dark loam with a thick stick. "Nothing here," he said, disappointed that his analysis had proven faulty. "I could've sworn —"

"Those satellite pictures weren't very helpful," Bootsie complained. She was getting hungry and that made her grumpy.

"Ikonos images are about as good as it gets," rebutted the boy. Not as cowed by adults as he got older. He was in the first year of his teens.

"How did you get access to those satellite images?" asked his grandmother, trying on a scowl.

"Uh, don't ask."

"I'm asking, young man."

"Grammy —" said Aggie.

Maddy gave her a stern look, a Medusa-turning-you-to-stone glare. "You stay out of this. I'm asking your cousin."

"Yes, ma'am."

N'yen knew he was backed into a corner. "I hacked into a company that uses orthorectified satellite imagery with extracted vector data and geospatial data to create geographic informations systems data-rich maps. It utilizes machine learning, neural networks algorithms and satellite remote sensing techniques to automate extraction of objects detected on satellite imagery."

"The only part of that sentence I understood was 'hacked,'" frowned his grandmother.

"Look," shouted Aggie. "Over here – a stone block!"

That shifted attention away from the boy. Everybody looked to where Aggie was pointing: a squarish brown stone visible through the wet leaves.

"We were just a few yards off," the girl said. "Wouldn't have seen it underneath these leaves, 'cept I stubbed my toe on it."

"I'll take a stubbed toe over a satellite picture," smiled Bootsie, her chubby cheeks looking like a chipmunk carrying acorns. She wasn't big on technology.

"The image was correct," pouted N'yen. "We were just off by a few feet."

Cookie leaned over to inspect the stone. She brushed away the dark leaves to reveal a second rectangular stone. And a third. "It looks like part of a foundation, but it's not made out of gold."

"You didn't take the inscription on that ring literally, did you?" laughed Maddy.

"Well –"

Bootsie spoke up, "It said, *The foundation of my home is golden.* That sounds pretty specific."

"That just means to look here in this spot," argued Maddy. "I think we're going to have to come back with shovels and dig."

"Not me," responded Lizzie, still standing on the

asphalt at the top of the embankment. "Let's call Darnell Watson to use his backhoe."

A local heavy equipment operator, Darnell Watson did snowplowing and dug septic tanks and gravesites. Watson was a roly-poly man with apple cheeks and thinning brown hair. Last week, he had dug the grave for Daniel Sokolowski at Pleasant Glade, the town's cemetery.

"Not a bad idea," Maddy admitted. "I'll pay to hire Darnell."

"Problem will be getting Boyd Aitkens' permission to dig up his land," Cookie reminded her. "He's not going to let us walk away with his gold."

"It's not his gold, it's mine," bellowed a deep voice behind them.

The women turned to face Jebediah Crackleton, standing next to Lizzie like a giant who had climbed down from his beanstalk. He looked very threatening with that snub-nose Smith & Wesson Model 327 in his hand.

CHAPTER TWENTY-FOUR
The Hit on Lizzie

"HERE'S THE DEAL," said Casper Crane. "A local socialite named Elizabeth Ridenour, that's who I want you to – as you so quaintly put it – whack. An older redheaded woman, they call her Lizzie. She's in charge of that new Quilting Museum on the south side of town."

Horace the Hammer cocked his head as the antiques dealer gave him the details. The two men had just agreed on $15 grand for the hit. Horace didn't plan on sharing it with that freak Maury Seiderman. He might do him in too, if he squawked about it.

"What's the item you want me to retrieve?" the burly man reminded his new employer.

"A quilt."

"Oughta have a lot of them at a quilting museum," he chuckled. Pleased with his little joke.

"Not just *any* quilt. You have to bring back a quilt made in 1830 by Ursula Andrea Jinks. She was the first wife of Ferdinand Jinks, one of the Town Founders."

"Big deal. What makes her quilt special?"

Crane grinned conspiratorially. "It's a treasure map."

Seiderman had been standing subserviently to one side. On hearing those magic words, the skinny man leaned forward, purplish eyes gleaming. "A treasure map? How do you know that?"

"'Cause I sold it to her – well, to her museum. But I didn't know what it was at the time. I was just getting rid of all the shop's quilting inventory. I don't know anything about needlecrafts. I can barely tell a patchwork quilt from a Cabbage Patch doll's blanket."

"Then how did you figure out you'd sold her a treasure map quilt?" pressed Horace Greeley.

"When I was cleaning out the back office, I found a journal. Turns out, my cousin Daniel kept a meticulous record of everything. Guess he didn't have anything much better to do, an old man in his eighties."

"He wrote about this treasure map in his journal?" Maury Seiderman's excitement showed on his narrow face.

"Seems he'd helped some local biddies look for a wagonload of gold that was hidden away in the early 1800s. They didn't find it and Daniel concluded it was just a baseless story that had been handed down through the generations. But then he came across this quilt."

"You don't say?" muttered Maury Seiderman.

Horace the Hammer was getting interested too. "Where did your uncle find this treasure quilt?"

"My distant cousin, not uncle."

"Cousin then."

Casper Crane winked. "Ol' Daniel bought the quilt from a Jinks relative who had inherited it from his mother. A guy named Louis Ritchie, he was trying to put together the money to buy himself a new airplane. Daniel paid him a thousand dollars for the quilt."

"Hey, I know that guy," exclaimed Horace. "Upside Down Lou, he's called. I sold him *my* plane, a sweet Cessna Turbo."

"But why would he sell a treasure map?" persisted

Seiderman.

Casper Crane looked like a tabby on catnip. "Ritchie didn't know the quilt was a treasure map. My cousin Dan figured that out. He was a smart old geezer. Gotta give him that."

~ ~ ~

Map Quilts are fairly rare. One of the earliest examples is an 1886 silk and cotton quilt with silk embroidery depicting the shape of the United States. The anonymous woman who stitched it was thought to be from Virginia.

The Quilts Exploration Guide states, "Although the map is an unusual treatment in the quilt idiom, there is a long precedent for depictions of maps on fabric. In the early nineteenth century, young women stitched sampler maps and three-dimensional fabric globes as part of their geography lessons. Few examples of pieced quilts in the form of maps exist today, however."

Map Quilts are generally considered a form of Show Quilts. Unlike traditional bed quilts, a Show Quilt is not composed of three layers (top, filling, backing) and in fact isn't quilted. A Show Quilt is designed to be placed on a bed for decoration or draped over the back of a sofa, but it's never meant to be slept under or laundered.

Many such quilts are wrongly cataloged as Crazy Quilts because they sometimes share the same characteristics as Crazies (e.g. foundation piecing, luxurious fabrics, and embroidery embellishments), but they are not randomly patched pieces of fabrics like a Crazy.

Lizzie would have categorized this one as more of a

Pictorial Quilt than a Show Quilt or Crazy Quilt. Crazy Quilts have no specific pattern. And Show Quilts didn't depict a geographic location. The difference between most historic Map Quilts and Ursula Jinks's 1830 example is that hers turned out to be an X-marks-the-spot treasure map like you'd expect from a pirate.

Well, not exactly an X, but close enough.

CHAPTER TWENTY-FIVE
Badger Hound

JEB CRACKLETON POINTED the Smith & Wesson at the cowering women. It wasn't clear whether he meant to shoot them, or force them to dig for the treasure, or lock them away in the Hoople Cottage while he retrieved the gold and made a getaway. But no one got a chance to find out his true intentions because a gray streak erupted from the open door of the Toyota, the furry form of a dog, sinking its fangs into the calf of the tall, gangly threat.

"Owwwwww," screamed Crackleton, dancing on one foot, trying to shake the small canine from his leg. But Tige held on like a saw-toothed clamp.

At that moment Lizzie Ridenour swung her pocketbook with both hands, catching the assailant on the shoulder, hard enough to knock him off balance. She must have been carrying rocks in the Christian Louboutin tote, for he went tumbling down the bank head over heels, like a scattering of Pik-Up-Stix.

The S&W 327 went skittering across the asphalt, coming to a stop at Lizzie's feet. Delicately, she picked up the revolver and pointed it in the general direction of the downed man. "Reach for the sky," she sputtered. "I'm making a citizen's arrest."

"*Arf, arf, arf,*" echoed Tige.

~ ~ ~

Aggie's dog Tige was of unknown origin, but its lengthy body suggested some dachshund in his DNA.

A German hunting breed, the dachshund name literally means "badger dog." It was developed to flush out badgers and other burrow-dwelling animals. The flap-down ears, big paws, long body, and curved tail were deliberately bred into the dog. The ears keep seeds and dirt from getting into the short-legged hound's ear canals when running through tall grass. Its front paws are paddle-shaped for digging. The lengthy body extends deep into burrows. And the dog's sturdy tail is useful for hauling it out of a burrow should it become stuck.

Books written in the 18th Century refer to the dog as a *Dachs Kriecher* ("badger crawler"). Some historians claim the dachshund's roots go back to ancient Egypt, based on carvings that depict short-legged hunting dogs. However, Aggie's dog Tige merely went back to a sign on South Main Street that said, "Give this puppy a good home."

Last year N'yen had proposed that his Badger Patrol make Tige its official mascot, but Aggie refused the honor as a protest over its He-Man-Woman-Haters-Club approach to membership. Not that she wanted to go camping. She just didn't want to be told she couldn't.

Now Tige was licking Aggie's face, making sure his young mistress was safe from the bad man. Dachshunds are known to be more aggressive to strangers than other breeds of dog. And Tige was no exception.

Bootsie was on her iPhone to her husband. Deputy Hitzer was already on the way to the Hoople Cottage with full lights and siren.

Jebediah Crackleton had really screwed the pooch this time. Or vice versa.

CHAPTER TWENTY-SIX
Crazy Claude

GRANNY CRACKLETON HAD THREE KIDS – Jeb, Claude, and Faith Ann. With Jeb locked up in the holding cell of the Caruthers Corners Police Department, she called Claude to come manage the convenience store in his brother's stead. No one was sure whether threatening the Police Chief's wife with a pistol was a ten-day crime or a ten-month crime. Rather than using words like "felonies" and "misdemeanors," the Crackletons talked in terms of "time served." This was based on their long history with the law.

If Jeb was tall at 6-foot-11, Claude was wide, weighing in at 410. A tailor's tape measure would not reach around his waist. He and his brother were regular customers at the Big and Tall Men's Shop in downtown Indy. Claude looked like Humpty Dumpty before he fell off the wall. But like all Crackletons, he was a little cracked. He was convinced an alien lived inside his head; that he had been taken over like those Pod People in *Invasion of the Body Snatchers*. But he pretended to be normal, else those sanatorium doctors might take him away again. He didn't like electric shocks, whether that was the prescribed therapy or not.

Even at 98, Granny ruled the minor kingdom of Crackleton Corners like an empress. Having been a Jinks before she married Happy Howard Crackleton, she resented the fact that she didn't get the same acclaim as Beau Madison or Henry Caruthers for being descended from a Founding Father. Ferdinand Aloysius Jinks had been on that wagon train same as Beauregard Hollingsworth Madison or Jacob Abernathy Caruthers. It wasn't fair.

She worried she might be developing that Old Timers Disease people talked about on television. After all, she was getting old. And her mind wasn't what it used to be. She couldn't believe she'd overlooked that house ol' Ferdie had built on the river as a possible site for his hidden gold. Jeb's boys had been digging in the wrong place all these years. Now Boyd Aitkens was likely to get it all.

Drat!

According to the *Burpyville Gazette*, Boyd had hired Darnell Watson to excavate that spot on the banks of the Wabash for the buried treasure. In the meantime, he'd hired security guards to ward off any poachers. No way she was going to get her hands on it now.

Jeb had made a try for it, but he'd been thwarted by a 16-pound weenie dog. He was so incompetent. Not that Claude was any better.

When she saw a picture in the paper of the four women who had discovered the treasure site – those Quilters Club busybodies – she recognized one of them as the Historical Society lady who had visited her recently. That was the galling part: She herself had told them where to find that wagonload of gold.

Now all Boyd Aitken had to do – as the legal property owner – was dig it up.

Drat and double drat!

Sometimes Granny missed her late husband. Happy Howard would've known what to do, how to recover the gold that rightfully belonged to the Jinks family. Unfortunately, Happy Howard had drowned when he tapped into an underground river while digging a well. He'd been a water witcher and well digger by profession. You could make a good living doing that in this part of the country. Now she had to depend on Social Security and the generosity of her multitude of children, grandchildren, and great grandchildren. There might even be a few great-great grandchildren around, she couldn't keep track.

Granny yanked twice on the string that hung from her porch ceiling. Thanks to an elaborate network of waxed kite cord, it rang a bell in the convenience store across the street. Two rings meant, Deliver a Red Cola. When Jeb's son Dub ran the store, he'd been prompt in his response. Despite his short legs, the dwarf could deliver an icy cold soda within five minutes. But due to Claude's elephantine size, it took him nearly 20 minutes. Or maybe he just didn't try to hustle, having an obvious lazy streak.

So she sat back in her rocking chair and waited.

~ ~ ~

Maury Seiderman had returned to the Evergreen Inn, carrying an armload of packages. He'd stopped at a construction site and stolen two sticks of dynamite. He didn't have any blasting caps, but figured he could set them off with an egg timer and a couple of batteries to provide an electric spark. He intended to wipe out those aliens who had given him an anal probe at Burpyville Memorial's Outpatient Clinic.

145

The way he looked at it, he was a soldier in an interplanetary war. Humans vs. Aliens. Damn those wily Grays, invading the earth without firing a shot. He was onto them.

Building the bomb would give him something to do while Horace Greeley took care of that Quilting Museum lady. The Hammer didn't need any help from a gimp with a sprained ankle. Horace could strangle her and be back at the motel with the Map Quilt before Maury could tie his shoelaces.

Maury Seiderman didn't entirely trust his newfound friend. Horace *was* a crook after all. And he was about to kill his second person within two weeks. That wasn't the best reference a guy could have.

Still, to collect $5K without lifting his finger was good fortune – for him, but not that Ridenour lady. Too bad she had to be collateral damage in getting that quilt back. Couldn't have her going around squawking about it. And on top of that, he was getting a 10% cut of the gold when they dug it up. Casper Crane had promised him that.

Sure, Horace was getting twice as much for the murder and a bigger share of the gold, but that was okay. Horace was the one doing the dirty work. Maury didn't have anything against killing someone, although he'd never actually done that deed himself. Aliens didn't count, of course.

Maury Seiderman spread out his paraphernalia on the cigarette-scarred side table in his motel room – sticks of dynamite here, timer there, Duracell 6v lantern batteries directly in front of him – ready to rock 'n roll. As he gazed down at his bomb materials, he suddenly realized he'd forgotten to buy wire. He needed electrical wire to connect the batteries to the timer and the dynamite.

He didn't know much about explosives. Dynamite was a tubular package of wood pulp soaked in nitroglycerin and nitrate. Setting it off seemed simple. He'd seen enough of those Road Runner cartoons where Wile E. Coyote ignited it with a match and a fuse. Should he have a fuse?

Where did you buy a fuse? A hardware store? Wal-Mart's? Home Depot? That might be a problem.

Blowing up invaders from outer space was more difficult than he'd expected.

PART IV

CHAPTER TWENTY-SEVEN
Gold Rush

CRANE'S ANTIQUARIAN ATTIC was located only a few doors down from the Caruthers Corners Police Department. The two buildings were separated by Cozy Café and the DQ, so when Casper Crane stepped over to the Café for a pick-me-up cup of coffee he couldn't help but notice the commotion taking place in front of the Police Department.

"What's going on?" he asked Maisie, the woman behind the counter.

"Jeb Crackleton just got arrested." Running a restaurant in a small town, she got news faster than the *Gazette*.

"Who's that?"

"Granny Crackleton's oldest boy. He owns that convenience store up on 101. They're saying he pulled a gun on my sister and the Police Chief's wife. The dumb cluck. All them Crackletons got a screw loose."

Crane ordered his cup of Maxwell House, a bargain at 50¢. It and watermelon pie were the Café's big draws – although pork tenderloins and Van Camp's pork and beans might be added to that popularity list. "Why did this Crackleton guy draw a gun on those women?" he asked as he sipped the lip-burning coffee. Strong, black, and hot – just the way he'd got used to drinking it in the teachers' lounge back at Brandon P. Semple Middle School in Ohio.

"Seems the Quilters Club discovered a hoard of

hidden gold. Buried by Ferdinand Jinks, one of the Town Founders. Ol' Jeb was trying to hijack it."

Casper Crane felt his heart skip a beat. "The, uh, Quilters Club?"

"Yes, that's a local quilting bee – mainly my sister Maddy, Lizzie Ridenour, Cookie Bentley, and the Police Chief's wife Bootsie Purdue. They have a bit of a reputation as amateur detectives, sniffing out crime and such. Buried gold, in this case."

"They found the gold," he muttered.

"Well, they haven't actually *found* it yet. But they've found where it's supposedly buried."

Holy Toledo! thought the antiques shop owner. If the location of the treasure had been found, he didn't need to kill that Ridenour woman for the quilt. Was it too late to call off Horace the Hammer?

~ ~ ~

Boyd Aitkens gave an interview to Ralph Wrightson, the reporter from the *Burpyville Gazette*. Wrightson's piece made the late edition, getting a place on page 2A. The town was abuzz with talk about the discovery of gold. You would have thought this was Sutter's Mill, California, circa 1848.

Somebody said there was a run on shovels at Home Depot, although the gold was in theory located in one small spot on Boyd Aitkens' land by the river. To protect himself from overzealous neighbors, Aitkens had hired three security guards to protect the old Jinks homeplace around the clock.

One of the guards was Metea Davis, that Indian who was night watchman at the Industrial Park. He took the morning shift, coming there straight after

work. The other two guards Aitkens got from Iron Fist
Enterprises, a private security firm out of Indianapolis.
Iron Fist had assigned Rex Blouderman and Tom
O'Brien – known internally as Agents X-3 and X-5.

Normally, Boyd Aitkens would have relied on Iron
Fist for all three guards, but he had a soft spot for Davis,
a genuine Potawatomi Indian. In times past, all of
Aitkens' land had belonged to the Potawatomi. Maybe
he had a touch of guilt, an unspoken recognition of the
settlers' role in plundering the land once known as
Indian Territory.

Unlike X-3 and X-5, Metea Davis refused to carry a
firearm. He didn't believe in brandishing the weapon
that had all but wiped out his forbearers. But he was
physically fit. Maybe he wasn't trained in Taekwondo
or Judo like those Iron Fist men, but he was adept at
Okichitaw, a Native American fighting technique. Not
that he expected to use it. Most people just gaped at
him as they drove by on River Road, taking in the newly
posted sign that warned:

PRIVATE PROPERTY
ARMED RESPONSE
FOR TRESPASSERS!

Armed response indeed! Metea Davis chuckled to
himself. In his case, that probably meant he'd have to
arm-wrestle any trespassers who wandered onto the
property.

~ ~ ~

After Deputy Pete Hitzer took the prisoner away,
Maddy loaded everyone into her Sequoia to ferry each
of them home. First in line, she dropped Lizzie off at

the Hoople Quilting Heritage Museum to pick up her car. It was 6 o'clock when the Toyota SUV pulled up to the front door. Before Lizzie retrieved her Mercedes-Benz from the museum's parking lot she wanted to make sure her docents had properly locked up.

"C'mon in," the redhead invited her friends. "I want to show you some of the quilts I got from Dan's Den of Antiquity."

"You mean Crane's Antiquarian Attic," Bootsie corrected her with a kidding wink. They were still getting used to ol' Daniel's absence. Acknowledging the new name was part of the process.

Everybody dutifully followed Lizzie into the building. Tige clicked along behind them, welcome in Lizzie's domain. She was a dog person. Cookie, on the other hand, maintained a strict NO PETS policy at the Historical Society's new home in the Perricock Museum of Science & History. Tige was no exception, much to Aggie's consternation.

Lizzie's tolerance was partly due to losing her Chihuahua recently. Chi Chi had been 18, fairly elderly for a canine. She had bought a small crypt for Chi Chi in a corner of Pleasant Glades, the town's cemetery. Although officially it wasn't a "pet cemetery," the corporation that owned it (MFP, Inc.) was quite mercenary, willing to bend the rules when enough money was put on the table. As heir to the Bergamachi fortune, Lizzie wasn't about to skimp on the proposition that her Chihuahua would be waiting for her in Heaven.

"Back here," beckoned the museum's director, leading them to the big vaulted-ceiling gallery where the new collection was on display. There were 22 quilts in all, about half of them Amish. Hanging over the entrance to the gallery was the famous Renaissance Quilt, the museum's prize exhibit.

"Wow!" said Maddy, surveying the room. The way the quilts were arranged around the high-ceiling space was impressive. Suspended from wires, like a fleet of magic carpets, the display forced viewers to look up at them. Others were displayed on wooden racks. Lizzie always had a flair for interior design.

"Nice," nodded Aggie.

"*Arf*," echoed Tige.

N'yen said, "Do you have anything to drink. I'm thirsty."

Lizzie pointed to a side door. "There's a small refrigerator in my office. Help yourself to a Coke Zero." The slender redhead had always been a Tab drinker, but one had to make do in these Troubled Times.

N'yen preferred the real sugar in Coca-Cola Classic (35g, or about 7 teaspoons) as opposed to the aspartame and acesulfame K found in Coke Zero Sugar. It was confusing to him that Coke Zero Sugar contained no sugar.

As the boy stepped into Lizzie's office he came face-to-face with a threatening-looking man, a burly individual with a flat nose and steely-gray eyes and a mouth that looked like an upside-down U. "Who are you?" he asked the strange man.

"Your worst nightmare, kid," growled the intruder, pushing the boy back into the main room.

"W-what's going on?" stuttered Lizzie upon spying the twosome.

"Get away from that boy!" ordered Maddy, taking a step forward.

The man flashed a knife. "Stand back or I'll slit the kid's throat," he replied in a menacing tone.

"Don't you dare," screamed Aggie. Her eyes narrowed to angry slits. "Sic 'im, Tige!" she shouted.

Upon command, the small fuzzy dog launched himself into the air like a missile from a catapult, seizing Horace the Hammer's wrist in his sharp teeth, causing the startled man to drop the blade. And at the same time, N'yen kicked the man in the shin, causing him to yelp and dance on one foot.

With all this distraction, Bootsie Purdue stepped forward and spritzed the intruder in the face with pepper spray, all but blinding him. As the police chief's wife, she never ventured out without a vial of Sabre 3-IN-1 in her pocketbook. Advertised as "Police Strength," the pepper spray promised up to 35 bursts from distances of ten feet.

Cookie was already dialing 911.

"Good dog," said Aggie, scratching Tige behind a floppy ear. The little mutt was getting good at this.

CHAPTER TWENTY-EIGHT
An Exclusive Interview

RIGHT NOW RALPH WRIGHTSON was driving down 101 like a Mario-Andretti-on-steroids maniac, heading toward Caruthers Corners, hoping to get a behind-bars interview with Horace the Hammer before the Feds took over. His sources said the FBI would be pulling rank, grabbing the case out from under those hick cops.

Deputy Evers Gochnauer stopped Wrightson for speeding just inside the town limits, wrote him an $80 ticket, then escorted him to the police department with lights blinking and siren blaring. As such, Wrightson got there a good hour before Special Agent in Charge Neil Wannamaker.

With Deputy Gochnauer at his side, Ralph Wrightson walked straight into the police department as if he had a Willy Wonka Golden Ticket in his hand. Nodding at dispatcher Myrtle Dobbler, the woman who played gatekeeper, he asked Gochnauer to take him straight to the prisoner. The deputy guided him through the door that led to the two holding cells as if he were a visiting dignitary.

"Here you go," said Deputy Gochnauer. "Horace the Hammer in the flesh." So wrapped up in his seeming power, Gochnauer didn't think to check with the Chief – an egotistical oversight that would get him a week's suspension without pay.

"Mr. Greeley," the interloper began. "I am Ralph Wrightson of the *Burpyville Gazette*. Could I have a few minutes of your time?"

Horace the Hammer smirked. "Help yourself. I expect I've got a little time available −45 years to Life, I'd guess."

"Just a few questions," the reporter said, switching on the digital recorder secreted in his jacket pocket. "Why did you kill Edward Benjamin Williams?"

Horace the Hammer stepped closer to the bars, causing Wrightson to inadvertently move backward, well out of reach. "Slick Eddy had it coming," said the prisoner. "He was a rat."

"Who was Williams going to rat out?"

"That's for me to know and the cops to find out."

"You were flying the plane?"

"I enjoy flying," nodded Horace Greeley. "Like to take junkets to Vegas. With my new Cessna Turbo I can make it with one stopover in Kansas City."

"I thought you sold your Cessna to a man named Lou Ritchie ..."

Horace frowned, wiggling his mouth to one side in a distorted frown. "Oh yeah, that's right. Upside Down Lou, he got the bargain of a lifetime – a $450,000 aircraft for 30-cents on the dollar."

"You're upset about that?"

The prisoner raised his thick eyebrows as if the answer to the question surprised even him. "Naw, good for Lou. He helped me in my time of need. And it looks like my flying days are over."

"So you pushed Edward Williams out of your plane over Never Ending Swamp?"

"Sure, why not admit it. There were witnesses. Some dame and two kids. Like I say, Slick Eddy had it coming. Told him we were going for a little ride where we could talk in private, not worry about the Feds wiretapping us. He fell for it like the *schmuck* he was. Going over the swamp I said, 'Look down there, a herd of reindeer.' He bent forward to check it out and – *whoops!* – out of the plane he went. Easy as pushing your pal off a diving board."

"Reindeer?"

"Made him look."

"And you tried to kill a local museum director?"

"That's what got me caught. Otherwise, I'd be gone like a ghost."

"Why were you attempting to murder this – what's her name? – Elizabeth Ridenour?"

"A local yokel name of Casper Crane paid me 15 G's to whack her. A simple business transaction. Shoulda stayed in my hidey-hole at the Evergreen. Woulda been safe there."

"Is it true that you were captured by a 10-pound dog?"

"That bowser musta been 40 or 50 pounds. Maybe more. Came at me like a rabid wolf. Didn't see 'im 'til he was on me. But it was the police chief's wife what got me, squirted me in the face with pepper spray. Nearly blinded me. I may have a lawsuit for excessive force."

"Is it true that you kneecap people for Sal Milano?"

"Hey, I've admitted to a murder and a half. Let's leave my lesser crimes out of this."

"But –"

"And I don't know nobody named Sal, got that?"

An hour later, digital recorder in hand, Ralph Wrightson went sailing out the front door to find a quiet spot to phone in his story. He practically collided with a tall man in a charcoal gray suit.

The sharp-faced man paused to squint at him. "Don't I know you?" said the FBI's Special Agent in Charge Neil Wannamaker.

"Don't think so," replied the reporter. "Worst crime I've ever committed was speeding." He held up the ticket as Exhibit A.

"You're that reporter —"

"You got me," Ralph Wrightson winked, then bustled toward his car.

The *Burpyville Gazette* was going to owe him a bonus for this one, ol' Ralph told himself. And he could sure use it. Relying on his pitiful newspaper wages, he was two months behind in his rent. What's more, that $80 speeding ticket would be coming out of his own pocket.

But things were starting to look up. Scoring an exclusive interview with the guy responsible for the Skydiver Murder was a heckuva coup. The killer had even confessed and he had it recorded on the Sony ICDPX in his jacket pocket. With any luck, he could be up for an AP award for investigative journalism. Wouldn't that be something, a two-bit hack like him!

CHAPTER TWENTY-NINE
An Alien Inside His Head

CLAUDE CRACKLETON REMEMBERED Granny's stories about a spaceship landing in the grassy field just south of the crossroads. He was convinced that's when the alien had taken over his body. People always said, "Claude, you're big enough to have two people in there." Little did they know.

He wasn't sure whether the pod person inside him had done a mind melt or not, tapping into his very thoughts and fears. But he wasn't taking any chances. He'd purchased a small battery-powered device guaranteed to scramble your brain patterns so they could not be read by aliens from outer space.

As it happened he'd bought the useless gizmo from a website operated by the Greater Midwest Occult Phenomena Association. He would have been very impressed if he'd known the founder of G.M.O.P.A. had been here in Crackleton Crossing only two days ago talking with his mama.

Claude had been acting a little strange lately. He blamed it on alien interference with his brain waves. That gizmo didn't seem to be keeping the voices out of his head. Claude's sister Faith Ann Ritchie was worried about him, but Claude was too big for his 98-pound sibling to handle. So she phoned her son Louis over in Burpyville and asked him to come check on his uncle.

Granny was surprised to see Upside Down Lou pull up in his open-top Cadillac. He didn't come around much, like he was ashamed of them or something. But he had Crackleton blood coursing around in his veins just like the rest of them. Behind his back she called him Uppity Lou.

Upside Down Lou strode over to the porch of Granny's shack, but didn't bother coming up the steps. "My mom says Uncle Claude's off his feed. Thought I'd take him over to Burpyville Memorial for a checkup."

"Who'll run the convenience store with both him and Jeb gone?" she complained.

"Ain't my problem."

"Will be if you have to start supporting your mama. Jeb gives her an allowance out of the store's funds."

"Y' mean out of his loansharking. Guess that's not going so well with him locked up in the hoosegow. What was he thinking, pulling a gun on the police chief's wife and her friends?"

"He was trying to claim what's rightfully ours – the Jinks gold."

"That's just an old wives' tale. You've spread that story so much, you've started to believe it yourself."

"No, it's true. I've got your great grandfather's ring to prove it. Says there's gold buried at Ferdinand Jinks's old homeplace."

"You and the boys been digging up the place for years. It's a wonder Boyd Aitkens hasn't had all of you arrested for defacing his property."

"When we get that gold, I'm gonna cut you out of your share. This ain't no way to talk to your elders."

"Sorry, Granny. But somebody has to maintain a clear head around here. The Crackleton Curse affects about ever dad-blasted one of you. I keep hoping it turns out I was adopted."

"Ha! The Curse will kick in at its own good time. They'll be saying you're 'cuckoo for Cocoa Puffs' too."

"Heck with it. Just tell me where to find Uncle Claude and I'll be gone. I'll bring him home tonight unless they decide to keep him."

"You know they'll put him back in the sanatorium and zap him with those electroshocks. If he ever does come back, his brain will be scrambled like it's been through an eggbeater. He won't be no help with the store."

"Maybe Jeb will be outta jail by then. I heard his pistol wasn't even loaded."

"Before you pick up your Uncle Claude, go by your mama's house an' tell her she had to come mind the store. Somebody's gotta bring me my soda pop when I ring the bell."

~ ~ ~

After scoring an exclusive interview with Horace Greeley, Ralph Wrightson got around to talking with Agnes Tidemore, the 15-year-old girl whose brave dog had gotten the better of two bad guys in one day. Using his Canon EOS digital SLR, he snapped a photo of her sitting next to her scrappy little pooch, a shot that had a good chance of making the front page. The blonde girl was very photogenic; her doggie was cute as a button.

It was amazing that a tiny 16-pound wire-haired dachshund mix had been able to overcome these guys — one a literal giant, the other a suspected killer who was thought to work for the mob. Maybe it was like they say about dynamite coming in small packages.

The reporter already had the angle figured out for

his story: He'd cook up a controversy, claim that some townspeople want to give the dog a medal, while the animal shelter wanted have him put down for biting two people. No, technically it wasn't true, but it would sell papers. Alternate facts. But by the time anybody sorted it out, he would have a nice bonus in his pocket. That's the way the newspaper game was played, coming up with a sensational hook to snare readers.

CHAPTER THIRTY
Hero Dog or Dangerous Cur?

AS PRESIDENT-ELECT of the Caruthers Corners Animal Shelter, Bootsie Purdue felt up to the task. Her husband was chief of police. Wasn't an animal shelter just a jail for wayward dogs?

No, Lizzie explained. The shelter was merely a way station for dogs on their way to a Forever Home.

"Oh," said Bootsie having an epiphany akin to Saul on the Road to Damascus. She immediately set about phoning everyone she knew, determined to place each and every one of her canine charges.

The Animal Shelter only had 7 residents at the moment, and two of them were already spoken for by potential adopters.

There weren't many pet stores or puppy mills in this part of the state, so most people looking for a dog were happy to have a rescue. These pooches made loyal pets when they found a good home.

That's why Bootsie was livid when she saw the morning's paper. There on the front page was a picture of Aggie and Tige with a large headline declaring: **Hero Dog Threatened By Shelter**.

The article claimed that the Caruthers Corners Animal Shelter was planning to euthanize the dog for biting two people. According to the writer – a reporter named Ralph Wrightson – a spokesman for the shelter had said it maintained a "Zero Tolerance" policy on biting dogs.

That was bull hockey. First, all the volunteers with the shelter were women, so there was no spokes*man*. And there was no Zero Tolerance policy. This was a No Kill shelter, where dogs were fostered until they could be placed in good homes. Many of the fostering families kept the dogs for themselves.

Besides, Tige had helped save her life – not once, but twice!

When she reported this to Maddy, her bestie immediately called her son-in-law. Mark the Shark in turn called the publisher of the *Burpyville Gazette* to give him a "shot over the bow," as he called it. Nobody was going to put down the mayor's daughter's hero dog.

~ ~ ~

Metea Davis was sitting on the levy keeping watch on Boyd Aitkens' supposed treasure trove. A breeze rustled the oak leaves overhead. Birds chirped from perches along the river. The young Native American was fighting an impulse to nod off. He'd come here to Hairy Toad Bend directly from his job as night watchman at the Industrial Park and hadn't had any sleep in 20 hours.

Davis snapped his head up when he heard a car approaching. The tenth one this morning. Normally very few people used this stretch of River Road, but traffic had picked up considerably since that story appeared in the *Gazette*.

The mud-splattered green Buick pulled up opposite where Metea Davis sat. Between the car and seated man lay the flat ground where a few rectangular foundation stones had been exposed. The driver's window rolled down to reveal the bulbous countenance of Big-Nose Evans.

"Hey, kid," called Evans. "Whattaya doin' down there – fishing?"

"No, working. I'm guarding this property for Mr. Aitkens."

Big-Nose Evans wrinkled his brow. "Guarding it from what?"

"Trespassers." He pointed to the sign.

"Am I trespassing?"

Metea Davis stood up and crossed the flat ground, stepping around the foundation stones. "Technically not. You're in a car on a public roadway."

"Thought I'd better ask."

"What brings you out here, Mr. Evans? This is a fairly out-of-the-way place," the security guard inquired.

"Read in the paper that Boyd had found the Jinks gold. Wanted to see for myself."

"Don't know if there's any gold here, but Mr. Aitkens has hired me and a couple others to keep away any poachers."

Big-Nose scratched his head. His dark mop of hair was unruly as usual. "Don't know if you'd call me a poacher, but I wouldn't mind doing a little advance digging down there. I'd split anything I find with you."

Metea Davis smiled, a kind of ironic grin that saw the humor in white men. "If I wanted to steal some of Mr. Aitkens' gold I would have already done so. Why would I share it with you?"

"Well, it'd be the neighborly thing to do."

"Neighborly? Last I heard, you live up on Highway

21 near Aitkens Produce. That makes you Mr. Aitkens' neighbor. You don't live anywhere near me."

"Yeah, but —"

"You've had your look-see, Mr. Evans. Best move it along. You're blocking traffic."

"Blocking traffic? There ain't any other cars —"

"There will be. More sightseers like you."

CHAPTER THIRTY-ONE
Young Love, Maybe

AGGIE CUT ACROSS the Town Square, off to meet Bobby Elwood at the DQ. This wasn't exactly a date, she told herself. Just two classmates sharing a Watermelon Blizzard at the local custard stand.

Nothing her parents could complain about.

Prissy and Teddy weren't available. They had gone to Burpyville Memorial to visit his Uncle Mario, recuperating from a broken knee and a fractured skull. A couple of weeks ago Mario had tripped over a chair, according his statement to the police. The hospital always reported suspicious injuries. Chief Crenshaw suspected this was the work of Horace the Hammer, but Mario was sticking to his story.

As Aggie passed Cozy Café, she spotted Alexander the Great sitting on a trashcan behind the diner. The big cat hissed in the direction of Tige.

Aggie's dog had an uneasy alliance with Mrs. Warton's cat. Elsie Warton lived one street over from Cozy Café but her battle-scarred tabby liked to hang out behind the diner for the abundance of table scraps and mice.

Poor Tige didn't see many cats and was not quite sure what to make of this rugged feline. Was he prey or predator? Should he chase it or run? So he compromised by doing neither, walking carefully past the diner as if the cat didn't exist.

Elsie Warton's late husband Hank had been the

founder of Sons of Anthony Wayne, the statewide campers program. He had started the organization in 1978 as a protest to the Boy Scouts of America moving its headquarters to Irving, Texas. Hank Warton had been lobbying for the BSA to choose Indianapolis.

In 2013 Hank Warton retired from his role as President of the Sons of Anthony Wayne. Moving from Indianapolis, he and Elsie had settled in Caruthers Corners. Two years later he dropped dead from a heart attack while mowing his lawn.

Henry Charles Warton left $100,000 to the local Badger Patrol in his Will. That enabled the troop to build a modest clubhouse on a section of land donated by Ben Bentley. Ben had been the troop leader for the past five years.

As Brigadier General, Ben reported to the HQ in Indy. But truth was, they let him do pretty much as he pleased. Sons of Anthony Wayne wasn't much on formality or structure.

The Badger Patrol held four camping outings a year. And anyone who wanted could attend the annual jamboree at the Indiana State Fair grounds each Spring. Last year the Badger Patrol won the jamboree's Most Innovative Camper Award. The trophy sat on the mantle at the clubhouse, a two-foot-tall gold-plated statuette of ol' Mad Anthony Wayne.

Bobby Elwood had belonged to the Badger Patrol until just recently, progressing from Recruit to Patriot, the organization's rankings. The members of Sons of Anthony Wayne ranged in age from 12 to 16. Although still 15, Bobby had outgrown it when he discovered girls – Agnes Madison in particular.

Aggie felt special that Bobby Elwood had singled her out from all the girls in school. She'd never had a boyfriend before and was proceeding with the relationship nervously. Last week at the Multiplex he'd kissed her. What was that all about?

She had to admit she'd liked it.

Her cousin N'yen was jealous – not in a boy-girl sort of way, just that he now had competition for Aggie's time.

Having an IQ "in the stratosphere," N'yen had skipped a couple of grades and was in the same 9th-grade class as Aggie. Being so much younger than the other kids, he didn't have many friends other than her. He didn't play team sports. He was too small for football, too short for basketball, and too uncoordinated for baseball. The chess club bored him and he had no interest in band. He was a loner, except for Aggie.

As Aggie walked past the Cozy Café she could see Bobby Elwood waiting on at the round concrete table next to the DQ. He waved when he spotted her. She waved back and picked up her pace. She wondered when Bobby might kiss her again.

~ ~ ~

Brigadier Ben (that's what all the campers called him) was conducting one of the bimonthly Trailblazers Training Sessions at the Badger Patrol's clubhouse. The lesson this week was knot tying – square knots, half hitches, bowlines, figure eights, monkeys fists, and so on.

Lieutenant Colonel N'yen Madison was showing his proficiency at tying a sheepshank. A shank is a type of knot used to take up slack or shorten a rope.

The 1-2-3-4 steps are simple:

- Create a simple loop in the rope, so one leading

end is on top of the trailing end of the loop.
- Repeat this process further down the rope to create 3 total loops that overlap.
- Reach through the two outer loops and grab the middle loop, then pull outward.
- Once the middle loop is pulled through the outer loops, pull on the free ends to secure.

This produces a flattened loop that's held at each end by a half hitch.

N'yen complete his knot in about ten seconds flat. To him it was akin to solving a Rubik's Cube (but simpler).

There were 12 members of Badger Patrol, but two boys were missing today. Georgie Yager was home with a summer cold. Buddy Smyth had a dental appointment in Burpyville.

Ben hoped he'd have everybody here for the next Trailblazers Training. Metea Davis was going to demonstrate Indian tracking and trailblazing techniques. As a full-blooded Potawatomi, Davis professed to know many outdoor skills.

Ri-i-i-n-n-g.

Ben Bentley's cell phone startled the campers. The rule was to turn off phones, games, and other electronic gizmos during Badger Patrol meetings. But the Brigadier General himself was the culprit here, having forgotten to power down his Samsung Galaxy. His friend Jim Purdue had teased him for having a Galaxy after those recalls for spontaneous combustion, but Ben said it made a good survival device – a fire starter.

"Hello," he answered the phone. The caller ID said it was his wife, so he didn't dare ignore it.

"Sorry to bother you, Snookums, but I wanted you to know I'll be late getting home."

Snookums? Listening in on the conversation, the ten campers giggled.

"Any problem?" Cookie had driven down to Indy to meet with her counterparts at the Indiana Historical Society, finalizing details about loaning the Madison Meteorite for temporary display as part of its Indiana Experience exhibit. Founded in 1830, IHS maintains the state's premier archives on the history of Indiana and the Old Northwest.

"Traffic is at a standstill. Apparently, a bomb went off at some motel up ahead. Police have blocked off the roads. Nothing is moving."

"A bomb –?"

"That's what they're saying on the radio."

"Many people injured?"

"Nobody is sure. One man seems to be missing. I may be stuck here in traffic for hours."

"Be careful. Terrorists sometime carry off multiple attacks. Like they did in 9/11."

"Don't worry, Snookums. This doesn't seem to be a terrorist attack. The radio says the police think it was a mob hit."

"Maybe you should pull over somewhere and have yourself a cup of tea until traffic is moving again."

"There's no way to pull over. I'm stuck here in the middle of Binford Boulevard near the ramp onto Interstate 69. Don't wait dinner."

CHAPTER THIRTY-TWO
Just in Time

RALPH WRIGHTSON SCORED another big scoop on the explosion at Evergreen Inn. That probably saved his job. The publisher had been pretty steamed with him following the phone call from the mayor of Caruthers Corners. In retrospect, Ralph had to admit he might have taken a few too many liberties with that dog story.

Thank his lucky stars that some crazy bombmaker had blown himself up in a seedy motel on the outskirts of Indianapolis. Ralph Wrightson had pretty good "sources" within the Indy underworld. He received a phone call from the motel's manager before the smoke had cleared. There was always a quick $20 for every good tip that Wrightson received. Most of the lowlifes knew this and kept his number in their wallets. Right next to a condom and the business card for a handy bail bondsman.

Turns out, a homemade bomb had taken out a block of rooms on the second floor of the Evergreen Inn. The cheesy motel was thought to be owned by Salvatore Milano, but the paper trail ended with a company registered in the Cayman Islands. Of course, the motel manager wouldn't comment on that detail. Nobody ratted on Sal the Whisperer.

The Indy Fire Chief reported that the explosion had emanated from Room 202, rented by a marginal character named Maurice Seiderman. A Google search listed him as founder of a UFO research group in Chicago. Efforts to identify other members of the fringe organization had proved futile.

According to the FBI, there was a possibility the bomb had been intended for the occupant of the adjacent room, now known to be Horace Greeley. Greeley was in police custody in a neighboring town. It was alleged he was responsible for The Skydiver Murder. Also he'd apparently tried to kill that group of women and children at a Caruthers Corners museum, but had been subdued by a dog.

Ralph Wrightson phoned in the story just minutes before the *Gazette*'s deadline. This piece on the bombing got Wrightson the front-page position over the fold, the most coveted spot in a newspaper. It had been a Hail Mary that earned him a second chance with the publisher, a dyspeptic man who should have been a dry cleaner or a grocer, not a journalist. But Justin Nightley's father happened to own the Nightley Newspaper Group so Ralph had no choice but dance to his tune.

However, this bombing story was a game changer. The *Burpyville Gazette* was going to owe him big. And if this didn't get the *Indianapolis Star*'s attention, nothing would. He'd beat out the *Star*'s best reporters on this story. Maybe it would help him get his foot in the door. If he could score a job at the freaking *Indianapolis Star*, he'd be rolling in the Big Time!

~ ~ ~

The name of the section of the Wabash that Metea Davis was guarding made him laugh – Hairy Toad Bend. Local people thought it was a reference to some kind of amphibian, perhaps the *Anaxyrus fowleri*. But they were wrong.

The Forest Potawatomi language is closely related to that of the Ojibwe. The words "*gipagawe obiigomakakii washkitigweyaa*" translate as Hairy Toad Bend. But according to Metea Davis's tribal elders, the area's name actually comes from a reference to *memegwesi*, meaning "hairy-faced bank-dwelling dwarf." Little toad-like people who hid in caves along the river. Legends tell of a race of little people who avoided contact with humans. It was said that these *memegwesiwag* loved children and would take them away from bad or abusive parents. However, if spotted by an adult these dwarfs would wail and thrash and beg them not to say anything of their existence, promising to reward those who kept their word by helping them in times of need.

Sometimes Metea felt like a *memegwesi*, a dwarf hiding among the white race. He didn't have a beard, but he *did* love children. His best friends here in Indiana were Agnes Tidemore and N'yen Madison. If called on, he would protect them from bad or abusive people.

CHAPTER THIRTY-THREE
Hole in the Ground

AFTER SPENDING ALL MORNING digging a hole the size of a backyard swimming pool, Darnell Watson threw in the towel. "That's as deep as I can go without Scuba gear," he quipped, switching off the backhoe's engine. "I'm below the waterline."

Boyd Aitkens stood there watching as the muddy waters of the Wabash steadily filled the rectangular hole. Darnell had dug inside the parameters of the stone foundation, going as deep as a gravesite, but nothing had turned up other than a few rusty farm artifacts. And water.

"Where the heck is the gold?" the farmer muttered.

The backhoe operator shook his head. "Beats me. But it ain't in that hole."

"Dad-blame that Maddy Madison. She hornswoggled me, making me think she'd figured out where ol' Ferdie Jinks buried his fortune." Aitkens swept off his John Deere cap with a callused hand and threw it to the ground.

"Well, I'm gonna load up my backhoe on the truck an' go home. Not much more to do here."

"Yeah, thanks, Darnell. Send me the bill."

~ ~ ~

Aggie decided Tige deserved a reward for being such a brave dog, so she and N'yen trudged down to the Dairy Queen to buy him a hot dog. Tige followed at their heels, ignoring Mrs. Warton's cat who hung out at

Cozy Café, like a bum hoping for a handout.

Since N'yen had helped Tige overcome that Horace the Horrible – or whatever the bad man was called – Aggie decided her cousin also deserved a reward. She ordered five hot dogs, two each for N'yen and Tige, one for herself. Two 16 oz. root beers and one large curly fries completed the lunch.

They sat at the concrete table in front of the DQ and ate their foot longs. Tige finished off his two (and half of hers) in about 30 seconds. N'yen wasn't far behind.

Sunlight cast a dappled pattern on the table, its rays filtering through the trees. Main Street was lined with silver maples, the most common of the 243 distinct tree species found along Indiana's municipally managed streets. The aroma of mustard and freshly mown grass and poppies and peonies wafted in the midday air.

"Look," he pointed. "Isn't that Mr. Sokolowski's cousin?" She looked up, spotting Casper Crane as he unlocked the front door of the antiques shop and slipped inside, as furtive as a burglar.

There was a new Lexus parked in front of the shop. It still had the price sticker posted on the driver's side window. Had Mr. Crane bought a new car?

"Want to go down to the Antiquarian Attic and poke around?" proposed Aggie. "I wonder if Mr. Crane still has that 1892 First Edition of *The Adventures of Sherlock Holmes*. I always liked that book. Someday I'll own one."

PART V

CHAPTER THIRTY-FOUR
The Map Quilt

LIZZIE RIDENOUR WAS TIDYING UP the quilt gallery. Yesterday's kerfuffle with that Greeley goon had left things slightly askew. Jim's deputies had tracked muddy footprints all over the place. And a quilt rack got broken during the fracas.

She picked up one of the quilts to fold it, but paused to look at it more closely. This was a Pictorial Quilt, an appliquéd scene showing a winding river and a couple of houses.

Something about it caught her eye. What was it? One of the houses – it looked kinda like Herbert Hoople's stone cottage. Yes, the front door with two windows on the left, one on the right. And the chimney positioned in the same place. Naw, couldn't be. Surely it was just a coincidence.

Walking into her office, Lizzie checked the inventory list for the quits she'd purchased from Daniel Sokolowski's cousin. Here it was, Quilt No. 17. Attributed to Ursula Andrea Jinks, ca. 1830.

Hmmm.

She put the quilt aside and picked up the telephone and called the number for the Historical Society. Cookie Bentley answered on the first ring.

"What are you doing?" demanded Lizzie.

Her friend paused, then said, "Eating an egg salad sandwich at my desk. I brought my lunch today."

"I hate to ask, but can you come over here?"

"Where's here?"

"The Quilting Museum. There's something you need to see."

Cookie said, "Can I finish my sandwich first?" You could hear her chewing.

"Yes, but hurry."

"Mmum-umph-um," came the response.

~ ~ ~

Cookie was bummed with Lizzie Ridenour for insisting she drop everything and rush over to the Hoople Quilting Heritage Museum. There was no straight route from the Perricock Museum of Science & History to there. Besides, traffic was heavier at lunchtime these days. A new McDonald's had opened on Highway 21 and everybody was flocking to it like bugs to a backyard electric zapper. Cross streets were clogged with cars and pickups, drivers on their way to scarf down a Big Mac and skinny fries.

After sitting in traffic for two hours yesterday in Indy, this seemed like déjà vu all over again to Cookie. She was exhausted. That bomb had disrupted traffic on the north side of the city. Not getting home 'til ten, she'd missed dinner entirely. Sleep had been like the Princess and the Pea. As for her mood, cranky was an understatement.

"So what's the big deal?" the beleaguered historian asked as she came barging through the front entrance, pushing past the squeaky turnstile and heading for the big gallery where Lizzie was waiting.

"I need your expert opinion about one of the quilts I got when I purchased the inventory from Dan's Den of Antiquity. There's something odd about it." The redhead pointed toward the appliqué quilt with houses on it.

"Lizzie, you know more about quilts than anyone in the county," grumped the discombobulated blonde. "That's why you got this job as executive director of the Quilting Museum."

"That's true, I do know more about quilts than anyone else in this sweet little one-horse town," she acknowledged, oblivious to the egocentricity of her statement. "But I need a second opinion. Take a look at this quilt."

Cookie adjusted the wire-rim glasses on the bridge of her sharp nose and squinted at the quilt. "Okay," she said. "Exactly what am I supposed to be looking at?"

"The houses."

"Yes, so?" replied Cookie. "This is a Pictorial Quilt."

"Actually, I think it's a Map Quilt. That's a subcategory of Pictorial Quilts."

"This is a map?"

"Sort of. According to Daniel Sokolowski's notes, this particular quilt was sewn by Ursula Andrea Jinks, first wife of Ferdinand Jinks."

"The wife who got scalped by Indians?"

"The very one. She was married to ol' Ferdie at the time he supposedly buried the gold."

"So?"

"Look closer at this quilt. Don't you think that little house looks like Herbert Hooper's cottage?"

Cookie leaned closer, inspecting the fabric. "Hmm, nice appliqué work."

"Ursula Jinks was a good quilter. I've seen two other examples of her work — still in the hands of the family."

"I have to admit this *does* look like the Hoople Cottage," allowed Cookie. "Windows in the same positions. And this crook in the river could be Hairy Toad Bend. But what's this second house next to it?"

"That's got to be Jinks's first house. Where we uncovered the stone foundation."

"Maybe."

Lizzie said, "I think it proves we were on the right track. But before we go further with our speculation, let's call Maddy and Bootsie. They should be in on this."

~ ~ ~

Upside Down Lou drove his uncle over to Burpyville Memorial, where the corpulent man was checked into the psych ward. "Another breakdown, I'm afraid," said Dr. Emanuel Gottlieb, the psychiatric resident who had been treating Claude Crackleton.

"He seems to be hearing voices again," Lou Ritchie reported. "Says they're from an outer space alien living inside him. Nutty stuff."

"Auditory hallucinations are a common symptom of paranoid schizophrenia. People suffering from schizophrenia often hear voices that seem to be emanating from within their skull. A function of the disorder."

"But aliens?"

"Schizophrenics like your uncle don't differentiate between what's real and what's not."

"Is he dangerous?"

"Schizophrenics can be volatile and highly unpredictable, but if they're receiving the right medication they're not usually dangerous."

"How long you gonna keep him?"

"Probably not long. We just want to run a few tests and determine if his meds need to be adjusted."

"No way to cure him? A lobotomy or something."

"While there's no cure for schizophrenia, I think we can effectively manage your uncle with medication and supportive therapies. We'll try to get him back to normal."

"His 'normal' is whack-a-doo crazy."

"That's not a medical diagnosis we use," the doctor smiled tolerantly.

"What about the alien? Can you get rid of him? Call an exorcist or something?"

"Mr. Ritchie, aliens are not real," said Dr. Gottlieb, eyeing the man carefully. After all, he reminded himself, schizophrenia is a genetic disorder that tends to run in families.

CHAPTER THIRTY-FIVE
No Dogs Allowed

AGGIE AND HER COUSIN stepped into the antiques shop, Tige at their heels. The air conditioning was on high, adding a mausoleum chill to the air. Dust motes danced in the yellow sunlight streaming through the front windows. There was a musty smell, the kind that accompanied old furniture and second-hand goods.

Casper Crane stood behind the counter, next to the brass NCR cash register. The free candy that Daniel Sokolowski kept on the counter was no longer there. It had been replaced by a sign that said YOU BREAK IT YOU BOUGHT IT.

"Hello, Mr. Crane," said Aggie. "We were wondering –"

Casper Crane glanced up, alerted by the bell over the door. "No dogs allowed in the store," the thin man snapped when he spotted the pet.

"Mr. Sokolowski always let Tige come in here," Aggie responded, surprised by the unexpected edict.

"Check the sign on the door, young lady. This store is under new management. Rules have changed. Take that dirty mutt outside."

"Tige is not dirty," she said. "He got a bath just last night." Her dog had been muddy from his excursion to the banks of the Wabash. It took a good scrubbing to get the dirt and burs out of his wiry hair.

"Doesn't matter. Out – all of you!" He pointed a boney finger toward the door.

"But we're customers," protested the Asian boy. "I'm shopping for a gift for my second mother. She's coming back home."

"Good for her. Hope she had a nice trip. Now leave please."

"But I wanted to buy her a –"

"We're closed today. In fact, closed till further notice. I just came in to pick up a few personal items."

As it happened, he was here to grab his checkbook and clean the cash out of the big brass register. He'd heard about Horace Greeley's arrest and figured it would just be a matter of time before the mobster ratted him out. Better get out of town before the *gendarmes* show up, he told himself. To heck with this dusty old store and its used furniture and kitschy knickknacks. Simply take the money and run. With nearly half a million dollars inheritance, he figured he could relax on a beach in Belize or Brazil until things blew over. He'd already been to the bank to clean out the account.

"There's no sign saying you're closed," Aggie pointed out. She waved toward the door to indicate the absence of any notice.

"Don't tell me how to run my business, young lady. Get your filthy animal out of here or I'll call the police."

"Go ahead, call Uncle Jim if you want." She stood her ground, not concerned about the legalities of trespassing.

"Uncle Jim? You're related to the police chief?"

"He works for my daddy, the mayor."

Uh-oh, thought Casper Crane. He hadn't recognized the little blonde till now – the daughter of

Mayor Mark Tidemore. This wasn't good. "Listen, if you two come back tomorrow, I'll give you fifty percent off anything in the store."

"Why would you do that?" asked N'yen, suspicious of this sudden generosity.

"Call it a 'Going Out of Business' sale," he offered them a ghastly smile. His teeth looked as sharp as crocodile incisors. Not an expression that inspired trust.

"What would that Sherlock Holmes book cost?" inquired Aggie, pointing to a 5-stack barrister bookcase near the door.

"What book?"

"*The Adventures of Sherlock Holmes* by Arthur Conan Doyle. That one with a gray cover and gold lettering, up there on the top shelf."

Crane glanced at the oak bookcase, a 1910 Globe Wernicke. "You want that book? Here, take it," he growled, snatching the volume off the shelf and thrusting it into her hands. "Now go. Come back tomorrow and I'll give you more books, okay?"

Anything to get them out of his hair. They could come back tomorrow, but he wouldn't be here. He'd be on his way to South America where extradition treaties were not easily enforced.

As Aggie left Crane's Antiquities Attic, clutching the rare volume to her bosom, she turned to her cousin: "Why would he do that?" she puzzled.

"What? Kick us out?"

"No, give me an 1892 First Edition of *The Adventures of Sherlock Holmes*. Daniel Sokolowski had it priced at $3,000."

"Maybe he doesn't know what the book's worth."
"Or maybe for some reason he doesn't care."

CHAPTER THIRTY-SIX
Got it Backward

BOOTSIE PURDUE ARRIVED about ten minutes after Maddy. By then, everybody had agreed that the appliqué house shape on the Jinks Map Quilt had to be the Hoople Cottage.

"It sure does look like it," Bootsie said as she studied the boxy design of the appliqué houses.

Cookie nodded. "That means this shape next to it has to be the Jinks homeplace, the spot where we found that old stone foundation."

"That would be my guess," agreed Lizzie.

Maddy didn't speak right away, biting on her lower lip as she examined the quilt. She was thinking. Then, brushing a sprig of silver hair from her eyes, she said, "I think we may have it backwards."

"B-backwards?" sputtered Cookie. "What the heck are you talking about? This quilt confirms everything we've been saying. Ferdinand Jinks built a house on the banks of the Wabash, his wife Ursula recorded it on this contemporaneous quilt, and the gold should've been there under the foundation that we uncovered."

"That's assuming there was any gold in the first place," said Bootsie, showing her growing discouragement. Always a glass half-empty gal.

"Well, it's certainly not there now. Edgar called earlier to tell me that Boyd Aitkens gave up. He didn't turn up anything valuable," interjected Lizzie. With little else to do, the retired bank president had walked down River Road to observe the excavation. The way a guy with idle time might stick his face through a viewing port in the wall around a construction site.

"No gold?"

"Afraid not. Darnell Watson dug about six feet down before water started filling up the hole. So he loaded his backhoe onto his truck and went home. Nada to show for the efforts. Unless you count a rusty horseshoe and the tines of an old pitchfork."

"Maybe it washed away in a flood," supposed Cookie, looking for a reasonable explanation of the gold's absence.

"Or somebody got to it first," offered Bootsie. Always looking at the dark side of the human heart.

"Or maybe we had it all wrong," shrugged Lizzie. "We wouldn't be the first to do that. Those Crackletons have been digging over at the other Jinks place for years."

"Not wrong, just backward," Maddy repeated.

"Okay, Miss Smarty Pants, what do we have backward?" Cookie responded with exasperation. As director of the Historical Society, she liked everything to be documented and factual. An orderly mind, she sorted the cans of food alphabetically on her kitchen shelves.

Maddy wasn't offended. She was used to Cookie's persnickety ways. "I don't know if the gold's there, but we need to look at the foundation of the Hoople Cottage."

"Why there?"

Because I think we got it backward. The Hoople Cottage was the original Jinks homeplace. The building next door –" she pointed to the second boxy shape on the quilt – "was just an out building, a stable. That's why Darnell unearthed a horseshoe and a pitchfork."

"What?" said Cookie. Bending over the quilt for another look: A winding swath of blue silk to represent the river. Two fabric houses positioned next to each other. Green trees shapes appliquéd to the light-gray cotton background. A wide silk binding to finish off all four borders.

"Maddy could be right," admitted Lizzie. "The Hoople house has more detail than the other one, suggesting it was the more important of the two buildings. And the door on the second building is much wider."

"Hmm," said Bootsie. Squinting one eye to examine the patterns. She needed prescription glasses, rather than relying on dollar-store readers. "So if this is a Map Quilt, shouldn't there be some clue pointing to the hidden gold?"

Maddy was standing to one side as Lizzie held up the quilt, displaying it for her confederates to see in its entirety. With a wide silk border, the house shapes occupied the quilt's center.

"Maybe there *is* a clue," smiled Maddy.

"How so?" frowned the police chief's wife. "I don't see anything."

"Neither do I," Cookie confirmed.

Lizzie's green eyes narrowed, holding her words.

"Look on the back," instructed Maddy.

Lizzie turned the quilt to display its verso. "Nothing here – blank."

"Wait," said Bootsie. Owl-eyed behind her 325+

magnifiers. "Isn't that a little yellow dot? Right there, see?"

Cookie put her nose practically against the batting, adjusting her spectacles on the bridge of her nose. "Yes, there is." She ran her finger lightly across the surface of the quilt. "It's a separate piece of fabric, an appliqué. About the size of a sequin."

"Now," Maddy instructed, "match up that yellow dot's position with the other side of the quilt."

With Lizzie holding the Map Quilt high, Cookie pressed her finger against the dot. Bootsie put her finger against the bump Cookie created on the other side of the thin quilt. "*Eureka!*" the pudgy brunette exclaimed. "Exactly opposite the front door on the Hoople Cottage."

"If that's the case, the gold's probably buried under the front stoop of the Hoople Cottage," surmised Lizzie.

"I think we're going to have to start calling it the Jinks homeplace," the bespectacled blonde historian announced.

CHAPTER THIRTY-SEVEN
Sweet Revenge

N'YEN HAD QUITE A TEMPER, although he was pretty good at hiding it. Nonetheless, his anger at being ejected from Crane's Antiquities Attic boiled to the surface like a pot of water left on a burner.

Or maybe the boy was just irked that Casper Crane had given Aggie a $3,000 book, but he had emerged from the shop empty-handed. He might be a genius, but his emotions were often those of a socially retarded child.

"I'm going to report him," announced N'yen as they walked past Cozy Café, only a few steps from the concrete bunker that served as the town's police department.

"For what?" asked his cousin, hugging the rare volume tightly. Her dog was close underfoot, avoiding Mrs. Warton's cat. The battle-scarred tabby lurked nearby, standing vigil over the row of trashcans behind the diner.

"You can't kick customers out of your store for no reason," he argued. "There's gotta be a law against that."

"I'm not so sure about that," the girl said. "I've seen signs saying a place reserves the right to refuse service to people who don't wear shoes or shirts."

"I have on shoes and this is a very nice shirt." It was, a new Lacoste stretch cotton piqué polo. He was proud of the smiling green alligator logo on the breast pocket. His Grammy had bought it for him only last month.

"You're wasting your time," she warned. "Uncle Jim has more important things to do than arrest shopkeepers for being rude to customers."

"We'll see about that. I might know something else about Mr. Casper Crane that the police would find very interesting."

"Watchoo talkin' 'bout Willis?" teased Aggie. She knew the television catchphrase irritated him.

"Come along and hear for yourself," N'yen said, veering toward the police department's front door. "I'm going to file a citizen's report of suspicious activity."

~ ~ ~

As Lou Ritchie left Burpyville Memorial through the front door, his Uncle Claude was departing by the ER's side entrance. Claude had simply walked out while his doctor was making arrangement with a nurse for his room assignment.

Claude Crackleton knew he couldn't stay there in the psych unit because they would subject him to shock treatments. He didn't like 450 volts shooting through his brain. Not only did it hurt, the jolts aggravated the alien who lived inside his skull.

Electroconvulsive therapy was introduced in 1938 as a means of inducing seizures in a patient suffering from severe depression or schizophrenia. Psychiatrists believe that mechanically produced seizures can modify the metabolism of the neurotransmitters that cause severe depression. ECT's effectiveness is debated. Side effects include amnesia, confusion, recurring seizures, brain damage, even cardiac arrest.

Claude had undergone electroshock treatments two times in the past. He wasn't worried about the side effects so much as he feared disturbing his embedded Martian. He didn't want to be pushed out of his own body into a state of nothingness, leaving the alien in his place. His brother Jeb wouldn't care, but his sister Faith would likely miss him. They had been close since childhood.

Making his way to the parking lot, Claude crawled into the back seat of his nephew's big 2004 Cadillac XLR. At 410 pounds, the man took up the entire seat. He pulled a car blanket over the mountain of his body, trying to hide. But it did little good. He was hoping Lou might report back to Granny Crackleton, thus giving him a ride home.

Anyone who looked into the back of the Cadillac convertible would have seen this oversized stowaway. But Upside Down Lou was so stressed he didn't give it a glance. He slid behind the wheel and screeched out of the parking lot onto State Road 31 without any further thoughts about the nutso relative he'd just left in doctors' care.

However, instead of going back to Crackleton Crossing, Lou drove his Caddy straight to the regional airport and parked next to the hangar where he stored his new Cessna Turbo 172 Skyhawk JT-A. He'd only flown the plane once since buying it from that low-level mobster. Nothing relieved stress like flying up there among the clouds. He estimated he had a good five hours of daylight left. Maybe he'd take 'er up for a quick spin. That would improve his mood f'sure.

Lou Ritchie ambled over to the airport office to let

them know he'd be taking his plane out for a short flight. He could already feel his blood pressure lowering in anticipation.

Now alone, Claude tried to get out of the Cadillac, but had trouble extricating himself from the backseat. He was wedged tighter than an oversized egg in a hen's butt. After lots of wiggling and twisting he managed to tumble onto the tarmac with a mighty "*oomph!*"

Painfully climbing to his feet, the obese man wandered into the hangar to get out of the sun. He took a deep breath, shook his head to clear away the yakkety-yak voice of the alien, and looked around. He found himself standing next to an airplane, close enough to reach up and touch the propeller.

He was pretty sure this was the new Cessna his nephew had bragged about all the way from Crackleton Corners to the hospital. It was a sleek beauty. He ran his hand along the polished fuselage.

Curious, he opened the cockpit door and leaned forward to look inside. To his eyes, the instrument panel could have been that of a Buck Rogers spaceship. An intimidating jumble of knobs, buttons, screens and levers covered every centimeter of the dashboard. He'd bet the extraterrestrial hiding inside his head could understand all those screens and knobs. But to him, they were a mystery.

Wanting a closer look-see, Claude tried to pull himself into the cockpit of the plane, but gravity worked against his gargantuan body. He fell backward, clutching for purchase as he went down. His left hand grabbed a bundle of wiring under the yoke, but his fingers slipped off. He landed with a *crack!* of earthquake proportions.

"Ooooow," he moaned, lying there on the concrete floor of the hangar. His breath had been knocked out of him. His back hurt. He was seeing double. Two planes. Two hangar windows. Two side doors.

After several turtle-like attempts, he struggled to his feet. He waddled up to the plane to shut the door. Wouldn't do for his nephew to know he'd been here. Better to let Lou think he was back at the psych ward. As he was closing the pilot-side door, he spotted a tangle of wires hanging down under the instrument panel. He'd accidentally pulled them loose. No, that wouldn't do. Carefully, he tucked the wires back up to where they wouldn't show. There, no harm done.

He heard voices. Was it airport mechanics – or his nephew returning? Or was it the alien inside his head? Looking around, Claude spotted a side door in the hangar. Without hesitation, he shuffled out the door and across the grassy apron toward the nearby highway.

About then, the gravelly voice in Claude's head shouted: "Run, run, run. They will catch you and pump your brain full of electricity. We don't like that. Electricity hurts!" But weighing nearly a quarter of a ton, his speed was about that of a walrus. *Grunt, grunt, grunt* – he plodded forward at his fastest pace.

Claude headed toward the traffic on State Road 31. Maybe he could hitch a ride back to the Crossing. He and his alien had no intention of going back to the hospital for another round of electroshock therapy.

Meanwhile, Lou Ritchie walked into the hangar with a member of the ground crew. They inspected the

Cessna. The plane had been fueled and was ready-freddy. Lou climbed into the cockpit and fired 'er up. The marshaller signaled him forward and guided the plane onto the runway.

Lou revved 'er up, cleared his take off with the tower and climbed into the sky. The weather was beautiful, the horizon clear. No air traffic in the immediate area. He leveled off and turned westward. Why not fly up to Caruthers Corners and take a look-see at Never Ending Swamp where Horace Greeley had dumped that guy, Slick Eddy Williams. While he was up that way he might even buzz Granny Crackleton's house just for the fun of it. No doubt the old biddy would claim she'd been attacked by a squadron of spaceships.

Lou rarely flew in this direction, sticking more to the south where his Drop Zone was located. His skydiving students wanted to ride the air, not waste their time on lengthy plane trips. As he approached Never Ending Swamp, he was reminded of its vastness, a tangled wilderness inhospitable to human penetration. He flew low, looking for the spot where Slick Eddy hit the ground, but nothing was visible through the thick canopy of trees.

Making a wide circle he passed over Gruesome Gorge, a zigzag gash in the ground below. Then he buzzed Crackleton Crossing, barely clearing the tin roof of Granny's boxy little house. He could see her sitting on the front porch, drinking a soda pop. She dropped the bottle when the plane came over, its landing gear nearly clipping her rusty roof.

He laughed like a madman as he pulled up and

headed toward the Wabash, aligning the Cessna's nose with the serpentine outline of the river. He liked the way his new plane handled. It'd been a good buy.

~ ~ ~

Casper Crane thought he was heading toward the Indianapolis International Airport, the large commercial airlines facility just southwest of Indy. By telephone he'd booked a Delta flight to Cancún, Mexico. From there he would go to Belize by boat. Muddying his trail in case the police tried to locate him. Horace Greeley was not to be trusted. The thug would likely trade him for a lighter sentence.

Problem was, the former Kacper Żuraw had no sense of direction. When a boy in Cleveland, he often got lost in his own Shaker Heights neighborhood. As a teacher he'd never mastered the maze of hallways at Brandon P. Semple Middle School. His students used to joke that "Mr. Crane could get lost in a phone booth." He'd had to rely on the GPS in his '98 Chevy to find his way home after school.

However, his new car – the 2018 Lexus LS 500 – came with a voice-activated Navigation System that could map millions of routes across the country and deliver the information in English, French or Spanish. But Crane did not know how to use it.

Crane had bought the car on a whim, giddy with his newfound wealth. He'd paid $75,000 cash on the barrelhead to Burpyville's Luxury Automobile Depot.

However, he'd purchased the Lexus before he knew Horace Greeley's murder-for-hire assignment had gone sideways. When he heard that Greeley had been arrested, he knew he'd have to skip the country. Of course, he'd tried to cancel the order, but Luxury Automobile Depot refused to refund the money. Greedy bastards! Like it or not, they'd delivered the showroom-new Lexus to him just this morning.

Now here he was on some back road that followed the river. Didn't the Wabash flow through downtown Indianapolis? He wasn't sure. But he hoped that by staying along the river he'd find his way to the state capital in time to catch his flight to Cancún. He would abandon the one-day-old car at the airport. A cost of $75,000 for a two-hour drive – that must set some kind of record!

Calling an Uber would've been a lot cheaper.

CHAPTER THIRTY-EIGHT
The Original Jinks Homeplace

THE QUILTERS CLUBBERS drove out to the Hoople Cottage – or as they were now calling it, 'the original Jinks homeplace.' There was plenty of room in Maddy's Toyota Sequoia without the kids. Cookie's husband had agreed to meet them there with a shovel and pick.

Ben Bentley was a short, powerful man, a farmer used to digging postholes and ditches and water wells. Retired, he spent much of his time volunteering at Haney Bros. Circus and Petting Zoo, but this was his day off.

Bentley was waiting for the four women when they pulled up at the riverside cottage. He'd parked his Dodge Ram on the shoulder of the narrow asphalt road, leaving the driveway open for them.

The cottage was looking a bit rundown. No one had lived there since Herbert Hoople's death a few years back. Shingles were missing from the roof. Several shutters sagged. The eves were in bad need of paint. It had that look of an abandoned house.

Maddy had got the scoop on the cottage by phoning her Aunt Hilda. As the last surviving member of the Hoople Quadruplets, Hilda headed up the family trust fund.

As Hilda told the story, the family's patriarch, ol' Hawthorne "Hatchet-Man" Hoople, had been a riding buddy of Ferdinand Jinks. That gave him dibs on prime real estate when this part of Indiana was being divvied up among the Founding Fathers. Hawthorne Hoople got Lookout Hill (now known as Hoople Hill) where he built a grand mansion. And when Ferdie Jinks gave up his original homestead on the river to move inland, he sold the modest structure to Hawthorne to use as a fishing cabin.

Hawthorne Hoople had put up a levy of sorts along the river, to keep the cottage from flooding. A few stray pilings suggested there had been a fishing pier off the levy at one time. This was an idyllic site, despite the stone cottage's rundown appearance.

The much larger Jinks mansion was located about a mile east of here on a parcel adjacent to the Madison farm. That had confused would-be treasurer hunters such as the Crackleton boys. Everybody had forgotten about the fishing cabin. When Boyd Aitkens bought up all these lands, reclusive Herbert Hoople was living in the fishing cabin, so that plat had been carved out for Herbie. Following his untimely death, the cottage reverted to the family trust fund.

"Ha!" said Cookie. "That means Boyd Aitkens has no claim on any gold under the Hoople Cottage."

"That'll surely tick him off," laughed Ben Bentley. Cookie's husband Ben was the second largest landholder in the county, his acreage only surpassed by Aitkens Produce. There was obviously a bit of competition between the two men.

"Does that mean the gold will belong to Maddy?" asked Bootsie. After all, Herbert Hoople had been Maddy's genetic father. She and her twin sister were now recognized as among the last of the Hoople lineage – although Aggie was making the claim that she and her sisters were actually last of the bloodline.

"No," demurred Maddy. "The cottage belongs to the Hoople Quadruplet Trust Fund. So if we find gold, it will belong to the foundation. And Aunt Hilda – through its administrator, Barnabas Soltairé – controls all that."

Soltairé was a former mob lawyer who'd given up his consigliere position to oversee the Hoople Quadruplets Trust Fund. His mother had been a long-time family retainer so the Hooples had put him through law school. Now he was paying his debts, so to speak.

Lizzie and Bootsie were poking around the structure's foundation, looking for any glints of gold. But there was nothing to be seen. Just mud-encrusted blocks of limestone.

Cookie was peering into the dark crawlspace under the cottage through a narrow opening in back. Given the high water table here on the edge of the Wabash, there was no basement. Just a two-foot space between the damp earth and wooden beams supporting the floor. Without a flashlight, she couldn't see squat.

Maddy circled the stone cottage like a realtor making an appraisal. As eagle-eyed as you'd find with any ASHI certified home inspection.

"Hey, everybody," called Edgar Ridenour from the top of the driveway. He'd hiked down to the cottage from his and Lizzie's imposing manor some three miles down River Road. He was getting used to it. "Found any gold yet?"

"Not yet," answered Cookie. "But Ben hasn't started digging."

"Hope you don't have to go down to the water level," Edgar chuckled. "You've already got one swimming pool." He nodded toward the water-filled hole that Darnell Watson had dug some twenty feet to the right.

"Not much danger of that," said Ben as he spit on his hands and rubbed them together. "Darnell used a backhoe. I'm using old-fashioned brawn. I'm not gonna try to outdo his heavy equipment."

Edgar looked around. "Do you have permission to be digging here?" he asked Maddy. Knowing she would be the ringleader.

"Straight from Aunt Hilda. If needed, Barnabas Soltairé will confirm that this is Hoople property."

Edgar couldn't help but laugh. "You mean Boyd Aitkens missed the gold by 20 feet?"

"That would be our guess," grinned his wife Lizzie. "Based on the Ursula Jinks Map Quilt."

"That one of your new quilts?"

"Yes, it was in that lot we got from the sell-off of ol' Dan Sokolowski's inventory."

"And you think the Jinks gold is buried here?" Edgar gave the old stone cottage a new appraisal, switching his assessment from money pit to a pit of money.

"Yes we do," came a chorus from the four women.

"Hey, where do you want me to dig?" asked Ben, eager to get started. Ready for sweaty work, he was wearing farmer's overalls and no shirt. The muscles on his back and shoulders stood out like ham hocks. He'd been a champion wrestler in high school and at 60 retained the physique.

"On the quilt the yellow dot was backed up to the

door of the cottage, so I'd say there," Maddy pointed. "Is there any way we can look under the stoop?"

Ben examined the stone slab that fronted the door. It probably weighed 600 pounds. "No way I can lift it," he said, "but if I hook a chain to my truck I can drag it away from the house."

Ten minutes later, a brown rectangle of dirt under the stoop was exposed. The stone slab rested three feet to the side, the chain wrapped around it like a metal ribbon.

"Let's see what we have here," said Ben, stabbing at the bared earth with his shovel, its blade sinking deep into the soft loam.

Nothing.

He turned another shovelful of dirt.

Nothing again.

"This is not looking good," muttered Bootsie.

The third shovelful came up empty too.

"Maybe the gold's somewhere else," posited Cookie.

"But where?" Bootsie looked around worriedly.

"I wish N'yen were with us," said Maddy. "He's small enough to check the crawlspace under the house without getting stuck."

"Do you think the gold could be buried in the front lawn?" speculated Lizzie, looking down at the unmowed fescue grass under her feet.

"Maybe," said Cookie. Looking doubtful.

"Don't you girls get any idea that I'm gonna dig up this entire yard," grumbled Ben Bentley. "I didn't sign on for that much work. You'll have to get Darnell back out here with his backhoe for that. I'll be happy to foot the bill."

As he made his pronouncement, the burly man stabbed his shovel into the ground with an abrupt downward thrust. Emphasizing his point.

Thunk!

The sound of the shovel blade striking a solid object.

"What was that?" said Lizzie.

"The treasure," smiled Maddy.

CHAPTER THIRTY-NINE
Fingering Mr. Casper Crane

N'YEN STOOD BEFORE THE DESK of Police Chief Jim Purdue – Uncle Jim, to him – giving his official statement. Deputy Viola Fahrner was writing it down. As the junior member of the force, she got all the scut work. She was transcribing the words carefully, for the small Asian boy had much to say:

> I, N'yen Madison, do hereby state that three days ago as I bought a Watermelon Blizzard at the Dairy Queen on South Main Street in Caruthers Corners, Indiana, I witnessed three men leave Crane's Antiquarian Attic, located next door to the ice cream parlor. I recognized one of the men as the antiques shop owner, Mr. Casper Crane. The second man was Mr. Maurice Seiderman, an investigator of alien phenomena from Chicago, Illinois. I had met him a few years ago when he threatened members of the Quilters Club with a gun. The third man was unknown to me at the time, but yesterday that same man also threatened me and a group of my friends with a knife. I have come to learn he is Mr. Horace Greeley, the accused murderer of Edward Benjamin Williams. I witnessed that very murder a week ago from the parking lot at Gruesome Gorge State Park. Today, I confirmed the identity of this third man by facing him in his jail cell in the presence of Police Chief Jim Purdue. This leads me to the conclusion that Mr. Casper Crane and Mr. Maurice Seiderman

were somehow in collusion with the alleged murderer, Mr. Horace Greeley.
(signed) *N'yen Madison*
in the presence of his guardian:
Beauregard Hollingsworth Madison IV.

Jim Purdue had called Beau after hearing the boy's story. Being that N'yen was a minor, Beau had to give permission for a more formal interview. He'd hurried over to the police department right away.

Even at 13 years of age, N'yen proved to be a highly credible witness. Sincere, clear, no discrepancies in his statement. His cousin Aggie stood to one side, mouth hanging open in amazement. She wished she had gone to the DQ with him that day so she could be a witness too. He was going to get all the glory.

As N'yen and Aggie rode back to Melon Pickers Row with their Grampy, the boy smiled to himself. "That will teach Mr. Crane to kick us out of his shop."

Arf, said Tige from the back seat, seemingly in agreement with that sentiment. His tail was wagging like a metronome.

~ ~ ~

By now Casper Crane was hopelessly lost. The road along the Wabash was narrow, hugging the banks of the river like a chalk outline. He'd seen no houses since taking this shortcut. Not a single place to stop and ask directions.

He pressed a button he thought might activate the Navigation System of the Lexus, but all it did was turn on the radio. A local news channel. Probably pre-set by the guy who had delivered the new car from Luxury

Automobile Depot.

"Top of the hour, we have a report that Horace Hammett Greeley, the accused killer in the so-called Skydiver Murder, has confessed to conspiring with a local businessman to murder Elizabeth Ridenour, director of the Hoople Quilting Heritage Museum, and steal a rare quilt. That co-conspirator has been identified as Casper Anthony Crane, owner of Crane's Antiquities Attic ...."

Holy jumping beans! Horace the Hammer had already rolled on him. There was probably a warrant for his arrest. Airport officials might already have be-on-the-lookout pictures of him. Indy police could be waiting for him at the Delta gate to Cancún. He felt his heart beating like a Spirit of '76 snare drum – *rat-a-tat-tat*. This changed everything!

His getaway route shifted in his reptilian brain. Instead of flying out of Indy for Cancún, he would drive to Chicago's O'Hare and catch a plane to Canada. Any place in Canada. Maybe he could lose himself in the Great North Woods.

But first, which way was Chicago?

At that moment, Casper Crane's car rounded a curve in the road, coming upon a small Hansel-and-Gretel cottage with a group of people standing around in the front yard. A blue Toyota SUV and a bronze Ram pickup were parked along the edge of the asphalt roadway. Maybe these folks could give him directions to the Windy City.

He pulled the Lexus over and rolled down the tinted-glass window. "Hello there," he called to get their attention. "Which way to Chicago?"

When faces turned his way, he was shocked to see those women from his cousin's funeral. And there in the middle of them was Lizzie Ridenour, the target of his wraith. She had bought the Map Quilt that Daniel Sokolowski's journal described as a treasure map. Too bad Horace had botched the job of killing her and retrieving the quilt.

But wait a minute! There was a muddy box at her feet, its lid standing open. Was that the glitter of gold inside? Had she and her Quilters Club cronies already followed the map to the Jinks gold?

Without giving it further thought, the skinny man slammed the car's automatic transmission into Park and pressed the latch that opened the glove compartment. From its roomy interior he pulled out the weapon he'd taken from the antiques shop – Bat Masterson's short-barreled Colt .45 with a gutta percha handle. It was loaded, ready to fire.

"Hand's up!" he shouted, waving the six-shooter at the people on the lawn.

The various individuals looked at each other, confused, then hesitatingly raised their arms into the air. Not sure what was going on.

"Casper, what do you think you're doing?" Lizzie confronted the intruder. "Put that gun down, you idiot."

"No way, you redheaded harpy. I want that gold. You used my quilt to find it." The Colt .45 didn't waver.

"Your quilt?" said Maddy. Staring him down. "Lizzie bought it from you fair and square, using a grant I gave to the Quilting Museum."

"You keep out of this, Mrs. Madison. I should've

asked Horace to kill all of you battle-axes."

Lizzie's green eyes flared. "You hired that thug to kill me?"

"You haven't heard the news? I'm all over the airways."

"Look," said Edgar Ridenour, "you can have this gold. Just take it and go." He didn't like the idea of his wife being threatened. Besides, they had lots of money. It wasn't worth dying for a pile of newly found gold.

Crane pointed the gun at Ben Bentley. "You, muscleman, lug that box over here and put it in my trunk." The press of a button caused the Lexus's trunk lid to silently rise like a leviathan opening it maw to be fed.

"I'll need some help," responded the farmer. "This box is pretty heavy. Two hundred pounds, I'd guess."

"Here, let me get one side," offered the retired bank president, eager to reduce the threat level.

The two men struggled to hoist the box of gold. There were no handles. Its sides slick with mud made it hard to get a grip. They found it quite heavy, the weight of the gold compounded by water sloshing around in the bottom of the old chest.

"Bring it over here," commanded Casper Crane as he boldly stepped out of the car.

~ ~ ~

Upside Down Lou was enjoying the handling of his new Cessna Turbo. That CD-155 diesel engine purred like a kitten. He watched the horizon, but kept one eye on the Attitude Indicator. Keeping her level, a smooth ride.

What the –? He knew something was wrong when

the plane gave a sputter and the wings in the Attitude Indicator tilted away from the instrument's artificial horizon.

The 6 basic flight instruments on a Cessna 172 are divided into two categories: Three instruments are connected to the aircraft's Pitot Static Pressure System, and the other three are Gyro Instruments. The Attitude Indicator uses a Gyroscope to stabilize a horizontal bar that stays parallel to the natural horizon. It shows whether the wings are level, and if the plane is climbing or descending.

Lou didn't get his nickname from safe flying, but usually when a plane banked it was because he intended for it to do so. Now, he had no control as the aircraft suddenly went into a downward spiral.

What the heck? He couldn't straighten her, couldn't pull her out of the spiral.

Time to bail out, he told himself.

Lou Ritchie was wearing a parachute, a common habit as a skydiving coach. Problem was, he was too low. There might not be enough altitude for the chute to deploy, much less grab some sky. But he had little choice. Every second brought the plane closer to the ground.

Elbowing his door open, he pulled up on the seatbelt's retractor and rolled his body to the left. Thankfully, the door didn't block him as can happen on a 172 Skyhawk. His feet had barely cleared the doorway when he pulled the cord. The risk was that the unfurling silk canopy or the suspension lines might catch on the landing gear, but luck was with Lou. The pilot chute pulled the skirt away from the plane and it popped open like a magic trick.

Even so, Lou was coming down fast. He knew he was going to hit the ground hard, maybe break a leg. Or worse. He hoped there were trees under him – the river was flanked with black gum, bald cypress, American beech, and chinquapin oak. A leafy bur oak would offer a better landing than a bed of river rock.

As it happen, he landed on top of Casper Crane.

EPILOGUE

THERE WASN'T a "wagonload of gold" buried under the stoop of the original Jinks homeplace; merely a small pitch-covered wooden chest filled with a number of 1 kilo gold bars. When people hear the term "gold bar," they tend to think of a fairly large gold brick like you see in a James Bond movie. But fact is, gold is so valuable that it doesn't take much to be worth a lot. A 1 kilo gold bar is about the size of an iPhone. Depending on the market value of gold, the 32.15 troy ounce bars would be worth around $43,000 each.

Unlike today's PAMP Suisse or Johnson Matthey commercially produced gold bars, the ones in the chest were not numbered or authenticated. The flat shapes were irregular as if smelted in haste. The bars were scattered in the wooden chest like uneaten Nabisco sugar wafers. By actual count, there were 53 bars in all, worth close to $2.3 million.

This was a pittance compared to the entirety of the Hoople Quadruplet Trust Fund, so Hilda Hoople instructed Barnabas Soltairé to assign it to the discoverers. However, the Quilters Club unanimously voted to divide the money between its two junior members, establishing college funds for Aggie and N'yen. For that kind of money, both kids could get advanced Ph.D.'s at an Ivy League University – and have change left over.

~ ~ ~

Louis Ritchie sprained his back from the fall.

Casper Crane had provided a fortuitous landing pad for the hapless pilot. Fortuitous for Lou, that is. Not so much for Casper who suffered a broken arm and a cracked collarbone. Being a part-time ambulance driver, Ben Bentley piled the two men into the bed of his Dodge Ram and drove them to the ER at Burpyville Memorial. Bootsie had called her husband, so Deputy Evers Gochnauer and his Burpyville PD counterpart were waiting for them at the hospital.

Greeley was arrested on suspicion of murder. Lou Ritchie was arrested for reckless endangerment.

Upside Down Lou collected $100,000 from his insurance company for the Cessna Turbo 172 Skyhawk JT-A. A $50-grand out-of-pocket loss. Depreciation, even though he'd owned it less than a week. The downed Cessna hit a silo on Abram Wagler's farm. Since Amish don't believe in insurance, Lou had to pay for the silo out of his $100,000. To make matters worse, Lou's pilot license was suspended for ten months. Hard to run a skydiving business without being able to fly.

Crane's Antiquarian Attic was sold to a chain out of Indianapolis. The company had 14 outlets throughout Indiana and Ohio, all operating under the name of Heirlooms Unlimited. The store was scheduled to reopen in a couple of months under the new logo. Fat Karl Schaeffer had been hired as the local manager. Turns out, Fat Karl knew something about antiques and collectibles.

After a sensationalized trial, Horace Hammett Greeley drew 65 years at Indiana State for the murder of Slick Eddy Williams. He got another 20 for conspiracy to commit murder, that sentence to be served concurrently. He denied knowing anyone named Salvatore Milano. But he unhesitatingly fingered Casper Crane.

Casper Anthony Crane got 20 years also. Initially he was on the same cellblock as Horace the Hammer at Indiana State, but got shivved during his first month of incarceration. Prison officials transferred him to the New Castle Correctional Facility where he recovered from his wound.

The FBI report stated that Maurice Seiderman died in the bomb blast, although no remains were found. As a minor player (and certified kook), nobody looked for him that hard. The Feds wrote Seiderman off as the unintentional victim of a bombing attempt on Horace Greeley, the mobster who'd occupied the adjacent motel room. Later on, there were reported sightings of Maury Seiderman in the Chicago area, but most people joked that he was on the lam with Elvis.

Jebediah Crackleton was released on his own reconnaissance; he ended up with a suspended sentence. He's back running the convenience store and doling out usurious loans.

Jeb's brother Claude is still under care at Woodmere (as Evansville State Hospital is known to locals). Opened in 1890 as the Southern Indiana Hospital for the Insane, the facility is one of several Indiana State Psychiatric Hospitals that provide medical treatment for chronic mental illness. Claude still hears the alien talking to him inside his head, but they've become friends.

The Jinks Map Quilt got a special display at the

Hoople Quilting Heritage Museum. A crowd of 80 turned up for the exhibit's opening. Not bad. Lizzie Ridenour's picture appeared in the Arts & Leisure section of Sunday's *Burpyville Gazette* along with a three-column article about the Map Quilt. A nice piece, it was written by Ralph Wrightson. A job offer at the *Indianapolis Star* had fallen through, but Wrightson got a raise at the *Gazette* after being nominated for an AP Investigative Reporting Award for his insider coverage of the Skydiver Murder.

Cookie Bentley and her husband Ben took a vacation to Cancún. She wanted to visit the pyramid at Chichen Itza. As a historian, pre-Colombian Mayan culture fascinated her. She took lots of pictures. Ben bought a llama for the Haney Bros. Circus and Petting Zoo. Shipping it back was a pain in the butt.

Figuring he'd go out on a high note, Jim Purdue announced his retirement as police chief of Caruthers Corners. He'd received credit for capturing the perp in the Skydiver Murder. As a result, he'd been honored as Indiana Lawman of the Year. Bootsie was very proud of her husband. But she was very busy these days with the animal shelter. She and Jim had adopted three dogs.

N'yen finally won his online game against Beelzebub666. It had been close. Even though a Buddhist, the boy still referred to his opponent as "The Devil."

When Aggie announced she was going steady with Bobby Elwood, her mother and father rolled their eyes, but said nothing, knowing that "high school romances" are often short-lived. Besides, everyone said Aggie and Bobby made such a cute couple.

As it turned out, Maddy Madison and Beau didn't have a happy ending. Their son Bill phoned to say he and Kathy would be driving down to Caruthers Corners next week to pick up N'yen. The boy would be going home with them to Chicago.

~ ~ ~

But before that happened, N'yen Madison (né Nguye n Van N'yen) was kidnapped by a person or persons unknown.

N'yen missing! That called for quick action by the Quilters Club.

Aggie took charge. Vowing to rescue her cousin no matter what it took.

But that's the next story.

Thank you for reading.
Please review this book. Reviews help others find
Absolutely Amazing eBooks and inspire us to keep
providing these marvelous tales.

If you would like to be put on our email list to receive
updates on new releases, contests, and promotions,
please go to AbsolutelyAmazingEbooks.com and sign
up.

Bonus

If you go to the Absolutely Amazing eBooks online bookstore (AbsolutelyAmazingEbooks.com) and enter the password below into the Bonus Reward Section, you can access recipes for many of the dishes you read about in this book – for free!

AA1059

About the Author

Marjory Sorrell Rockwell says needlecraft arts – quilting, crocheting, knitting – are pastimes every woman can appreciate. And she particularly loves quiltmaking. "It's like painting with cloth," she says. But when not quilting she writes mysteries about a Midwestern sleuth not unlike herself, a middle-aged lady with an unpredictable family and loyal friends. And she's a big fan of watermelon pie.

ABSOLUTELY AMA⚡ING eBOOKS

AbsolutelyAmazingeBooks.com
or AA-eBooks.com

www.ingramcontent.com/pod-product-compliance
Lightning Source LLC
Chambersburg PA
CBHW070837030726
47504CB00005B/1123